"I am not turning my life inside out for a temporary thing like…this."

"Temporary?" Anger sparked off him. "That's how you think of us?"

She turned her back on him, uncertain why tears were gathering in her eyes. "I've always said so, haven't I?"

"Then let it be temporary." Seizing her by the shoulders, he turned her to face him. "Just come with me for now. Better yet, commit the next few weeks to wherever this takes us."

A few weeks of this sweet torture? Longing assailed her, but that she wanted it so much was reason enough to shake her head. "No."

He cupped her chin in his hand and lifted her face, plumbing her eyes with his gaze. She closed them. "You're afraid I'll change your mind," he pronounced softly. She denied it, as she must. "You are," he refuted gently, "and you should be. Because I will."

Dear Reader,

Well, if it's true that March comes in like a lion and goes out like a lamb, you're going to need some fabulous romantic reads to get you through the remaining cold winter nights. Might we suggest starting with a new miniseries by bestselling author Sherryl Woods? In *Isn't It Rich?*, the first of three books in Ms. Wood's new MILLION DOLLAR DESTINIES series, we meet Richard Carlton, one of three brothers given untold wealth from his aunt Destiny. But in pushing him toward beautiful—if klutzy—PR executive Melanie Hart, Aunt Destiny provides him with riches that even money can't buy!

In *Bluegrass Baby* by Judy Duarte, the next installment in our MERLYN COUNTY MIDWIVES miniseries, a handsome but commitment-shy pediatrician shares a night of passion with a down-to-earth midwife. But what will he do when he learns there might be a baby on the way? Karen Rose Smith continues the LOGAN'S LEGACY miniseries with *Take a Chance on Me*, in which a sexy, single CEO finds the twin sister he never knew he had—and in the process is reunited with the only woman he ever loved. In *Where You Least Expect It* by Tori Carrington, a fugitive accused of a crime he didn't commit decides to put down roots and dare to dream of the love, life and family he thought he'd never have. Arlene James wraps up her miniseries THE RICHEST GALS IN TEXAS with *Tycoon Meets Texan!* in which a handsome billionaire who can have any woman he wants sets his sights on a beautiful Texas heiress. She clearly doesn't need his money, so *whatever* can she want with him? And when a police officer opens his door to a nine-months-pregnant stranger in the middle of a blizzard, he finds himself called on to provide both personal and professional services, in *Detective Daddy* by Jane Toombs.

So bundle up, and take heart—spring is coming! And so are six more sensational stories about love, life and family, coming next month from Silhouette Special Edition!

All the best,

Gail Chasan
Senior Editor

Please address questions and book requests to:
Silhouette Reader Service
U.S.: 3010 Walden Ave., P.O. Box 1325, Buffalo, NY 14269
Canadian: P.O. Box 609, Fort Erie, Ont. L2A 5X3

Tycoon Meets Texan!

ARLENE JAMES

SPECIAL EDITION®

Published by Silhouette Books

America's Publisher of Contemporary Romance

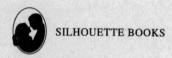 SILHOUETTE BOOKS

ISBN 0-373-24601-3

TYCOON MEETS TEXAN!

Books by Arlene James

Silhouette Special Edition

A Rumor of Love #664
Husband in the Making #776
With Baby in Mind #869
Child of Her Heart #964
*The Knight, the Waitress
  and the Toddler* #1131
Every Cowgirl's Dream #1195
Marrying an Older Man #1235
Baby Boy Blessed #1285
Her Secret Affair #1421
His Private Nurse #1482
***Beautician Gets Million-Dollar Tip!* #1589
***Fortune Finds Florist* #1596
Tycoon Meets Texan! #1601

Silhouette Books

Fortune's Children
Single with Children

The Fortunes of Texas
Corporate Daddy

Silhouette Romance

City Girl #141
No Easy Conquest #235
Two of a Kind #253
A Meeting of Hearts #327
An Obvious Virtue #384
Now or Never #404
Reason Enough #421
The Right Moves #446
Strange Bedfellows #471
The Private Garden #495
The Boy Next Door #518
Under a Desert Sky #559
A Delicate Balance #578
The Discerning Heart #614
Dream of a Lifetime #661
Finally Home #687
A Perfect Gentleman #705
Family Man #728
A Man of His Word #770
Tough Guy #806

Gold Digger #830
Palace City Prince #866
**The Perfect Wedding* #962
**An Old-Fashioned Love* #968
**A Wife Worth Waiting For* #974
Mail-Order Brood #1024
**The Rogue Who Came To Stay* #1061
*Most Wanted Dad #1144
Desperately Seeking Daddy #1186
**Falling for a Father of Four* #1295
A Bride To Honor #1330
Mr. Right Next Door #1352
Glass Slipper Bride #1379
A Royal Masquerade #1432
In Want of a Wife #1466
The Mesmerizing Mr. Carlyle #1493
So Dear to My Heart #1535
The Man with the Money #1592

**This Side of Heaven*
***The Richest Gals in Texas*

ARLENE JAMES

grew up in Oklahoma and has lived all over the South.
In 1976 she married "the most romantic man in the world."
The author enjoys traveling with her husband, but writing
has always been her chief pastime. Arlene is also the author
of the inspirational titles *Proud Spirit, A Wish for Always,
Partners for Life* and *No Stranger to Love.*

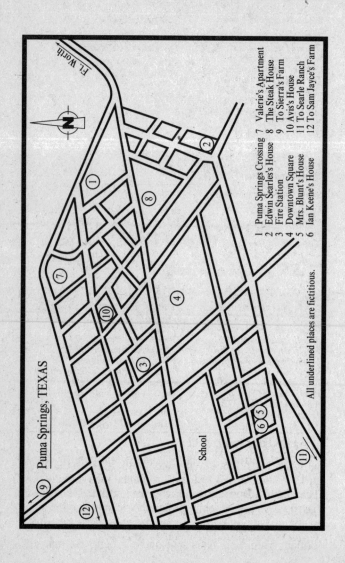

Puma Springs, TEXAS

To Ft. Worth

N

1 Puma Springs Crossing
2 Edwin Searle's House
3 Fire Station
4 Downtown Square
5 Mrs. Blunt's House
6 Ian Keene's House
7 Valerie's Apartment
8 The Steak House
9 To Sierra's Farm
10 Avis's House
11 To Searle Ranch
12 To Sam Jayce's Farm

School

All underlined places are fictitious.

Chapter One

"You're going to London?"

Avis smiled patiently at the clipped tone of her adult stepson and pushed back a silky, dark-brown curl which had escaped the butterfly clip at her nape, maintaining a soft and even inflection from long practice. "Yes. The flight leaves at three."

"*Today?*"

"This afternoon."

Ellis frowned at his coffee cup and folded his arms. "Well, that's just peachy."

He had arrived on her doorstep completely uninvited two days earlier. She supposed she shouldn't have been surprised, but it had been months since she and her friends Valerie Blunt Keene and Sierra Carlton had unexpectedly inherited just over a million dollars each, and Avis had naively believed that all of the kooks and moneygrubbers were already out of the woodwork. Apparently Ellis had needed some time to overcome his great resentment of her before the smell of hard cash could lure him to her door. Now here he sat on the other side of her breakfast table, a thirty-year-old self-described musician watching his opportunity to work her latent guilt wing its way across the ocean.

"Had I realized you were coming…" She let that thought hang, implying that her plans had been made before his arrival instead of during the predawn hours of that very morning. Perhaps if he hadn't made her so very uncomfortable she would not have taken such a drastic and unprecedented step, but the truth was that she did *not* want to play hostess to her truculent stepson.

Avis sighed internally. The world had turned upside down since Edwin Searle had passed away. No one had realized that the irascible old rancher had hoarded millions, certainly not the three women who had shown him little more than common courtesy and found themselves heirs to his estate. No one had been more shocked about that than Edwin's greedy nephew, Heston Searle Witt, who also just happened to be the town mayor.

Heston had gone out of his way to make the lives of the heiresses miserable since the reading of the will. Val was now happily married to Ian Keene, the town Fire Marshal, and they were expecting a child, but Avis shuddered to think what Heston would be saying about Sierra's situation, Sierra having only just revealed news of her pregnancy to a group including her very surprised boyfriend Sam. Avis felt a moment's uncertainty about her decision. Sierra might need her emotional support. On the other hand, Sam and Sierra seemed too happy about their impending marriage to care what Heston might say. They were being married quite soon in a private ceremony. They wouldn't miss her for a while, perhaps a long while.

Irritation flashed over Ellis's lean face. "I guess that's what I get for acting on impulse." He worked his narrow jaw consideringly. "How long do you suppose you'll be gone?"

"I really don't know," she replied smoothly, dipping a spoon into a cup of raspberry yogurt. It was the absolute truth. When she'd booked the flight around 2:00 a.m., she'd purposely left the return trip open-ended.

A muscle flexed in Ellis's jaw. "Can't your partner—what's his name? Colie?"

She looked down. Was it her fault if Ellis assumed the trip was business? "Coeli. Peter Coeli."

"Can't he handle this?"

Avis spooned the yogurt into her mouth, swallowed and carefully said, "He has too much to do already."

A respected real estate developer in the Dallas/Fort Worth Metroplex area, Pete had responded positively to Avis's proposal to join her in some modest development in the small town of Puma Springs, forty or so miles southwest of Fort Worth. Together they had rebuilt a burned-out office building on the town square and lured a convenience-store chain with its attendant jobs to a prime location on the highway. Pete had quickly offered her a limited partnership, and she had accepted, maintaining office hours in Fort Worth three days a week.

Lately the situation had become a little strained as Pete's manner had turned more and more flirtatious. He was a nice man whom she considered a friend, but as a widow of four years and now a woman of means, Avis treasured her independence. An ingrained gentility made it difficult for her to purposely hurt another's feelings, but she now considered that her impromptu decision to visit London might serve two objects. Three really. Not only would she escape Ellis, she'd put some distance between herself and her business partner, plus she had to admit to herself that this would fulfill a lifelong dream.

Avis had always wanted to see London. She imagined seeing Buckingham Palace and Westminster Abbey, envisioning Big Ben in the background. Belatedly, she realized that Ellis was speaking.

"So I thought I'd look for work in the Dallas/Fort Worth area."

Avis blinked. "I thought Austin was the great music scene."

He shifted uncomfortably. "Well, yeah, but I sort of need a new venue. You know how it is. Same old same old kinda robs you of your spark."

So that's how he intended to play this. She looked down at her yogurt and said gently, "I guess you'll be apartment hunting then."

"Sure. Eventually."

She dipped her spoon again and sweetly asked, "Staying with friends in the area?"

His face blanched, then pulsed bright red. "I don't actually know anyone else in the area."

"Oh, dear." She laid aside her spoon. "I hope you weren't planning to stay here. I'm only two years older than you. People will talk. You know how small towns are."

"But you're my stepmother," he argued.

"Was," she corrected faintly. "Oh, Ellis, I'm sorry, but it's just not possible."

Ellis pushed back from the table, saying bitterly, "I always knew you didn't want me around."

Avis tamped down an uncharacteristic spurt of impatience and imbued her voice with every ounce of compassion and empathy that she possessed. "That's not true, Ellis. When your father was alive, I would have welcomed you at any time. He missed you."

"He could've come home."

"You know that's not true."

"It would have been if he hadn't met you."

Avis sighed, aloud this time. She couldn't deny it, but shouldn't Ellis have come to some kind of peace with the situation after twelve, almost thirteen, years? When he'd first arrived, she'd hoped that he meant what he'd said about wanting to mend fences, but she'd quickly realized that was not the case. Ellis had hated her even before he'd met her, and that emotion still simmered just beneath his sullen surface.

She didn't blame him, actually, but what good could come from his punishing her? This was all about the inheritance. So long as she had struggled to eke a living out of her late husband's modest hobby shop, her stepson had been content to bank his resentment, but her incredible good fortune of being named in Edwin Searle's will must have been more than he could bear.

London not only seemed more compelling all the time, it was beginning to look like an absolute necessity, for Ellis's sake as much as her own.

She laid aside her napkin, eyes averted. "I'm sorry you feel that way, Ellis, and I wish I had more time to talk about this with you, but I must be at the airport by one."

"I could use some cash to get back home on," he told her bluntly.

She bit her tongue to keep from asking what had become of the two hundred fifty thousand dollars in life insurance he'd been awarded after Kenneth's death. Instead, she walked out of the kitchen and down the hall to the bureau in the entry, where she habitually left her purse. As she removed her wallet, Ellis walked up behind her. She quickly extracted a sheaf of bills, turned and pressed them into his hand.

"It's all I have on me at the moment, almost three hundred, I think. I hope that helps. Now if you'll excuse me, I have to get dressed."

Ellis stuffed the cash into the pocket of his jeans and made a begrudging attempt at politeness. "I could drive you if you like."

"No need," she replied with a smile, moving toward the stairs. "Besides, it's over an hour opposite to the direction you'll be traveling."

"Whatever," he mumbled, heading for the guest room.

Avis shook her head as she climbed the stairs. Ellis

might have seen thirty birthdays, but emotionally he was still seventeen. She couldn't help wondering if, had things worked out differently, his father might have been able to help Ellis grow up. The weight of that worry burdened her, but it was a familiar yoke, and she knew too well that nothing she could do now would lighten it. Ellis was Ellis, and that was that.

She turned her mind to the coming trip and felt a surge of excitement. Perhaps it was good that Ellis had come. He had given her the impetus to fulfill that dream. She and Kenneth had never had the money to travel together. Once the decision had been made, she hadn't been able to curb her excitement. Her bags were already packed. Now all she had to do was get herself ready. She started with a long, hot shower, mentally reviewing her "to do" list. Her passport, acquired some months ago, had to come out of the key safe in her downstairs office. She would likely need her laptop, too, since she and Pete really did have deals working, though nothing she couldn't handle via e-mail and telephone. On the way to the airport, she should stop off at an Arlington electronics store and pick up a voltage adapter so she could use her various personal appliances in England. Most importantly, she had to make a couple phone calls.

After blow-drying her thick, shoulder-length hair, glossing her full lips and applying a touch of taupe shadow and black mascara to play up her dark-blue eyes, she chose a smart knit pantsuit in an icy shade of lilac that seemed just right for the first Monday of April and made the most of her creamy pink complexion. The slim tunic top with its keyhole neckline and loose, bracelet-length sleeves lent the illusion of added height to her 5'6'' frame and played down her more than ample bust line, while the long, flowing pants promised comfort and a lack of bagging over the long transatlantic flight. A matching handbag and mules with gently pointed toes, a corded, low-slung belt and simple amethyst earrings completed the look, but she also took along a soft taupe cloak, with a hood in case of rain, to combat the cooler temperatures she was bound to encounter in Britain.

She spent the better part of an hour on the telephone, first with her good friend Gwyn Dunstan, who got the whole story, and then with her business partner Pete, who was shocked but evidently encouraged to hear that she "did have an impulsive bone after all." When she finally dragged her bags down the stairs, it was to find Ellis gone without so much as a farewell. She was not really surprised, but his abrupt departure did not change her mind about the trip.

After retrieving the necessary items from her office, checking the windows and appliances and rinsing the few breakfast dishes, she locked up and went on her way. Even as she negotiated the long drive to the airport, she enjoyed a growing sense of excitement. For the first time since the inheritance she was truly indulging herself.

She had been very sensible to this point, making her money work for her, keeping her expenditures within strict limits, protecting as much capital as possible and planning for the future. Now she was about to make a lifelong dream come true, and if she was doing it alone, well, she'd always been alone, really, even during her eight-year marriage. At twenty-seven years her senior, Kenneth had seemed wise and charming in the beginning, a respected professor at the University of Texas, but in the end he'd been more a dependent than a mate, especially after they'd discovered the cancer. Fully half her marriage had been consumed by that insidious disease and its debilitating effects. In the years since his passing, she'd been concerned with just keeping body and soul together—until Edwin had changed everything for her.

She had a real career now, and she was surprisingly good at it. With careful planning and execution, she could see her holdings grow exponentially. Never again would she have to worry about making a mortgage payment or babying her rattletrap car, which she had immediately replaced after receiving the inheritance. Old habits died hard, however, her new coupe was sporty but inexpensive. It had taken her some time to get to a place where she could allow herself something as carefree as this trip, let alone splurge on first class. Still, she couldn't bring herself to bypass the cheaper rates of remote parking.

Had she realized how difficult it would be negotiating the shuttle bus ride to the correct terminal with a whole carload of luggage, she might have changed her mind and parked in close. As it was, she doggedly pushed and pulled and toted, determining with every step not to let the inconvenience spoil the mood, until she got herself and her belongings to the ticket counter. From there on out, it was smooth sailing.

The counter clerk apologized for not being able to wave her through passenger security screening, as had apparently been the case with first-class passengers in the past, but Avis assured the woman that she didn't mind standing in line like everyone else. The whole thing took less than eight minutes, anyway. Little more than an hour later, she was following a pretty flight attendant with a long, golden ponytail down a wide concourse.

She stepped onto the jumbo jet with great curiosity and a quiet sense of awe. A few other passengers were already settling into place in the cabin. One man, a tall, handsome fellow with artistically tousled dark-blond hair already looked quite comfortable with a folded newspaper in one hand and a glass of red wine in the other. Everything about him proclaimed money, from the expert cut of his expensive suit to the Italian leather briefcase at his feet and the air of nonchalant authority spiked with complete confidence. As the flight attendant led Avis to her seat, he looked up from his newspaper. Surprisingly dark eyes swept over her, and her skin prickled as if electrified. She swept her gaze around the spacious cabin but couldn't help glancing at him again. He smiled slightly before going back to his newspaper, and heat bloomed instantly in her cheeks.

''Number six,'' the flight attendant said, stopping next to a comfortable leather chair. ''The seat next to yours is empty, so feel free to take the window seat, if you like.''

Avis smiled, feeling foolish. "Thank you."

Before the words were even out of her mouth, the attendant stepped across the aisle, hovered solicitously close to the dark-eyed stranger and inquired, "Can I get you anything else, Mr. Tyrone?"

The voice that answered her was deep, urbane and flavored with the faint spice of an accent. "I'm fine, thank you."

"My pleasure, sir. Call if you need anything, anything at all."

He lifted his glass in a wry salute and watched as the lithe blonde swayed down the aisle to greet the next, and as it happened, the last first-class passenger to board the flight.

Avis lifted a brow. Apparently some passengers were more first-class than others. Well, he was an attractive man. Extremely attractive.

She shook her head at such errant thoughts as she divested herself of her paraphernalia. The briefcase containing her laptop went onto the seat nearest the aisle. She tucked her handbag beneath the empty berth in front of it and draped her coat over the arm before seating herself next to the window.

The attendant returned to trade a pillow and blanket for Avis's wrap, which she promised to hang in a forward compartment where it could be retrieved handily at landing. Avis politely refused the offer of a glass of white wine and sat back to await take-off. As she did so, a sense of quiet satisfaction crept over her. She breathed deeply, relaxing, and felt exhilaration begin to build. It was a heady feeling, one she had never felt before.

No, wait. She had felt this before, this sense of being where she should be at the very moment she should be there, of being poised on the edge of a grand adventure. The memory crystallized for her.

It had happened on the third or fourth day of her second week at college. After days of confusion and uncertainty, she had finally found her bearings and known exactly where she'd been going as she'd walked briskly across the busy UT campus. The class to which she'd been heading, Natural Biology, had promised to be one of her least favorite, but had been required core curriculum for the sensible Business Management degree upon which she'd set her sights. Yet, she had felt then this same serene affirmation that filled her now. She had known that she'd made the right choice, was in the right place, doing the right thing. Even the sense of loneliness that she'd carried with her since the age of eleven, when her parents had been killed in a traffic accident, had briefly receded. In that moment, everything had seemed possible, even those dreams she had dared not voice.

It hadn't lasted.

The problems and choices of everyday life, not to mention biology, had soon swamped her, pulling her off course time after time, until finally her dreams were dashed upon the hard rocks of reality and consequence. Was it possible that she might actually find herself upon the right path, or was this just that moment of sweetness before the rug was yanked out from under her again?

History told her that it would most likely be the latter, but a hope that she hadn't realized she still possessed held out for the former. She laid her head back against the seat, content to rest in the moment in which she found herself, anticipating the excitement to come.

They were still loading the rear compartment when the Adonis across the aisle laid aside his newspaper, leaned forward and in that low, deep voice stated baldly, "You like to fly."

She turned her head, smiled politely and admitted, "I expect to."

His dark eyes flickered as he computed this information. "You have never flown before?"

"No. This is my first time."

She looked away, disturbed by the unwelcome distraction of senses alerted to anything but the anticipated experience. Closing her eyes, she inhaled deeply and silently, reaching for that rare moment again. Before she found it, the great engines of the jet rumbled faintly to life, and excitement slammed her heart against the walls of her chest. Gripping the curved ends of the armrests with her fingers, she realized that the clicking sounds she heard were the results of the other passengers fastening their seat belts. Delighted, she searched for and found both ends of her own. After sliding the buckle into the clasp, she pulled the belt tight across her lap and tried not to grip the armrests again.

An announcement was made over the intercom system. The only words Avis understood were "take-off" and "nine hours." Then the flight attendants directed the attention of the passengers to television monitors mounted to swing arms which pulled up from the sides of the seats. A video detailing emergency procedures played, but Avis could barely pay attention as the plane began slowly backing away from the terminal. She sat forward with great anticipation, gripped by an almost childlike zeal.

A low chuckle to her left told her that her embarrassing eagerness had been noted. She sat back determinedly. As the video finished, another announcement was made, this one very short. To her frustration, she didn't catch a single word. That's when her traveling companion spoke up again. She could hear his smile in his voice. It sounded…indulgent, knowing.

"According to the pilot, we've had a bit of good luck and will only be fifth in line when we reach the take-off queue."

As if to punctuate his pronouncement, the engines abruptly idled back. Deflated, she flashed a look in the stranger's direction. He abruptly leaned sideways and reached a long arm across the aisle, offering his hand and a very radiant, very white smile.

"I am Lucien Tyrone."

Something about that name sounded vaguely familiar, but she couldn't place it. Nevertheless, good manners made her stretch across the empty seat beside her. His warm hand gripped hers tightly. An intense physical awareness rippled through her, making her tongue stumble over the syllables of her own name.

"A-Avis L-Lorimer."

The flight attendant hurried toward them. She smiled at Lucien Tyrone, but she reached for the briefcase which Avis had left on the seat next to her. "Let me stow this for you before take-off."

"No, allow me," Lucien insisted, releasing Avis to take the briefcase from the hands of the flight attendant.

The attendant huffed slightly, then re-glued her smile and turned away. Avis tried not to widen her eyes at the very pronounced sway of her hips as she swiftly retreated.

"Let me know when you want this back," Lucien said, his lightly accented voice laced with delicate humor, the briefcase disappearing under the seat in front of him.

"Oh. Yes. Thank you. Uh, my laptop is in there, by the way."

"Ah. So this is a business trip?"

"Not exactly."

"But you can't completely leave the office behind, eh?"

"I guess you could say that."

"I only ask since you seem to be traveling alone."

She smiled but wisely did not confirm that, but then she didn't have to. It was obvious that she had boarded the plane alone.

"Perhaps you are meeting someone?"

"Yes," she lied, not quite able to meet his eyes.

He pursed his lips slightly, then said in a very relaxed, casual manner, "If this is your first flight, then I must assume you haven't visited London before. If that is where you are stopping."

"No. I mean, yes. That is, I have *not* visited London before, and that is where I'm…stopping."

A lazy smile tilted up one corner of his mouth. "You will adore London. I promise you." He said it as if it was a solemn and very personal vow.

Suddenly, without warning, the engines revved and the huge jet surged forward. Avis caught her breath, hands once more gripping the padded armrests. The beguiling man across the aisle laughed as the aircraft picked up speed and she caught her breath.

They raced on and on, faster and faster, until the massive vehicle shuddered and rattled. Then she felt a lift, surprisingly gentle, only to find herself abruptly pressed back into her seat as the nose of the airplane pointed skyward. She looked out the window and saw the ground falling away. Elated, she pulled in a breath of pure freedom.

They climbed for a long while, and she rode it out with enthralled relish, feeling her cares and burdens lighten as she traded sky for earth. Just before the big jet leveled off, something compelled her to turn her gaze across the aisle.

Lucien Tyrone smiled, his dark eyes glinting with satisfaction, indulging himself vicariously in her thrill, and then she was in that moment again, that rare instant when all is right with the world. Long seconds passed before she could make herself turn away, but even then the strange new sense of hedonistic fulfillment lingered.

Some dreams, it seemed, really did come true.

Chapter Two

Luc smiled to himself. Flying commercial offered unforeseen benefits. His finely tuned sexual radar had fixed on the scrumptious brunette even before he'd looked up from his newspaper, but he still hadn't been prepared for the quickening he'd felt at his first sight of her. The beauty of her oval face with its wide forehead and slightly pointed chin had momentarily stopped his heart.

Though not a classical beauty, her beige-pink skin and full, wide, rose-red lips were utterly perfect. An elegantly shaped nose, neither too long nor too short, added to the symmetry of a beauty that verged on the ethereal. Her eyes tipped the balance to the exotic side. Large, elongated and thickly lashed, their outer edges tilted upward slightly, lending her a nymphish air. He hadn't gotten close enough just yet to discover their actual color, but he would. Soon.

Patience, he counseled himself, sensing a certain protective aloofness about her, despite her fragile, soft-spoken manner. He could afford to take his time. After all, for the next eight or nine hours, they were both effectively trapped.

Luc was suddenly glad that his mother had commandeered his personal jet for a rush trip home to Greece and that every other vehicle in his private fleet had already been promised or was out of commission for one reason or another. This wasn't the first time that such a thing had happened, but in the past he'd always been able to charter air transportation, so it had been a shock to find that his usual sources were over-booked. Apparently charter services were in great demand, to the detriment of the beleaguered commercial airlines. In the end, the only expedient thing to do had been to book a commercial flight. He had viewed it at the time as a major inconvenience, especially when he'd discovered that he wouldn't even be able to get a direct flight from California. Then she had boarded the plane in Dallas/Fort Worth, alone, and in an instant, he had judged all his inconvenience worth it.

She was exquisite, this Avis Lorimer. Shapely, self-possessed and softly feminine with a voice like satin, she displayed an unselfconscious elegance. She was also skittish.

Either singleness was new to her or much too familiar. He had no doubt that she was single, and even suspected that she had lied about meeting someone in London, not that it mattered so long as she was unmarried. Satisfied that was the case, he signaled the waitress for another glass of the excellent red wine that he had had sent aboard from his own private stock and settled back to wait.

More than two hours passed before she grew tired of staring out the window. He frowned when she began checking out the in-flight movies, but then she put away the monitor and pulled out the airline magazine. He quickly leaned forward and offered his newspaper, a national daily. She turned a surprised, wary look on him, so he kept his smile perfunctory.

"Interesting article on foreign real estate investment."

"Oh?"

"The prices in London are astonishingly high."

"Are they? Guess it's a good thing I'm not in the market."

She glanced away, but her politeness made it easy to keep her talking.

"I was more interested in the article on the problems of the travel industry," he went on conversationally. "Difficult times. But at least we are doing our parts, you and I." He, actually, had been asked to do a great deal more by arranging long-term financing for one hard-hit major carrier. He still hadn't decided whether to get involved. Surprisingly, he found himself wanting to tell her about it. He quelled the urge. Discussing business with strangers was never wise. As she finally took the folded paper from him, he added, "Oh, and the weekly movie guide is in this issue."

"For London?" she asked doubtfully.

"No, but then I find that London is much more into live theater."

"Really? You seem to know a lot about the city."

It was all the invitation he needed. Having un-buckled his seat belt at the first opportunity, he rose and slipped across the aisle and into the seat next to her. She drew back, but he didn't let that stymie the conversation. "London has dozens of theaters of every description, many of them quite family-friendly. But then, consider the history."

She lifted an eyebrow. "Starting with Shakespeare, I suppose."

He smiled and pitched his voice low. "We could start earlier if you like."

Her eyes glinted with humor and gentle reproach. They were dark blue, almost solid in color. "I don't think that's necessary."

He chuckled. "All right. Let's just say that live theater seems always to have been among the great pastimes of the British. Do you know, they still send vendors down into the common in some houses to hawk treats during intermission? Live theater with ice cream and candy. It's rather charming, actually."

She had relaxed a little. "Sounds as if you've seen your share."

He nodded and quipped, "When in London…" She smiled at that, so he stayed with it. "I love the old theatres with their opera boxes and faded ele-gance, and even those little cubby holes where they cram mismatched tables and chairs into the room and pass out the ale. It's…I don't know, quintessentially London.''

"How do you mean?''

"Well, it's not like Greece, where the ancient is ever-present, or California, where if it isn't the hottest thing right this moment then it just isn't worth considering. London is connected as firmly to yesterday as to tomorrow.''

She stared at him for a moment. Then a shy smile curved her lips, and the lushness of that mouth, the *possibilities* of that mouth, kicked him brutally in the groin.

"You obviously know London well.''

Forcing himself to look away from her lips, he cleared his throat and tried to maintain the physical distance between them when what he most wanted was to lean in and let her essence swirl across his senses. "I know many places well.''

"So you travel a lot?'' He nodded, and she laid her head back against the seat, sighing. "I've always wanted to travel.''

"And now you will,'' he said, trying not to sound as if he was planning her future for her, which he very well could do, at least in the short term, if everything worked out as he hoped. But he was getting ahead of himself, way ahead. Best not to think beyond London. Yet his mind whirled through his schedule for the next several months: Buenos Aires, Bonn, Seattle, Toronto, Orlando, Chicago. He could always squeeze in Greece, too. Smiling at the picture forming in his mind, he asked mildly, "Have you ever thought of the Mediterranean?''

She just looked at him. Then she laughed, a smoky, feminine rustle that hinted at silken covers. She would make love with intense concentration, this one, and she was going to make love with him. She just didn't know it yet.

"Well, everyone's *thought* of the Mediterranean," she said in that smooth, honeyed voice. "Have I considered visiting that part of the world? No. Not really."

"You should," he said.

"And why is that?" she wanted to know.

He told her. Everything but the basic truth.

"I know what that's like," she said softly, glancing up at him from beneath her lashes. The conversation had come finally, almost inevitably, to this. "My husband died over four years ago."

He rubbed two fingers across one eyebrow. "It will soon be five years for my wife. I remember when it happened someone said to me that it was a great burden but also a blessing to be the one left behind. I look at my son, and I don't find losing his mother a blessing."

She felt a pang of grief for that little boy and wondered aloud, "How old is he?"

"Six."

"It must be difficult, traveling so much with a young son to care for."

He nodded but said, "I am fortunate that my mother is devoted to his care."

"He must miss you, though."

A shadow moved across his eyes, wistful but also

accepting. "Not as much as I miss him." He seemed to shrug off a touch of melancholy then and leaned closer to say, "I've never found any blessing in her death, but I'm no longer angry, and I'm glad to be with my son."

Avis nodded her understanding of that, feeling a deep empathy. "How did she die?"

"Such a simple thing," he said, spreading his hands. "A tumble down a ski slope. At first I thought she was playing. It was like her, always teasing, and she looked fine there in the snow, so pretty and peaceful, as if she was just gazing up at the blue sky. I could not believe that she was gone." He snapped his fingers. "It happened like that."

Avis shook her head. "My husband died inch by slow inch. Cancer."

He reached for her hand. The heat of those long, golden fingers shocked her, and she realized at that moment how cold she was. She shivered, and he pulled the blanket from the corner of her seat, shaking it out over her. It seemed an oddly intimate thing to do, and she glanced around warily. To her surprise, all the other occupants of the cabin seemed to be sleeping. Checking the window, she saw only black. They had been talking for hours!

"I'm glad Althea did not suffer like that," he said, tucking the blanket around her shoulders. His dark gaze, sooty black, touched hers and clung. Slightly breathless, she could only think that he had the darkest eyes and longest eyelashes she had ever seen. His hands tarried at their work a moment longer, then he sat back. "So you're going to London for a vacation."

She nodded, but she didn't want to talk about why she was vacationing alone, so she turned the tables on him. "And you for business. May I ask what type of business?"

He shrugged. "In this case, shoes."

"*Shoes?*" She shook her head doubtfully. "Somehow I can't see you as a shoe salesman."

He smiled lazily. "I am something of a—how shall I put it?—a freelance business manager."

She shifted in her seat, her scepticism lingering. "A *freelance* business manager?"

He chuckled and tapped a fingertip consideringly against his lips. Very fine lips they were, too, sculpted and firm. "Let us say that someone, a designer, perhaps, has a talent for creating things that others want to buy, but he has no talent for marketing those things, even though they practically walk off the shelves on their own. He is such a poor businessman, in fact, that no matter how wonderful his designs are, sooner or later he will find himself working for nothing, all his money going everywhere but into his own pocket. That's when I take over, show him how to make profit for both of us."

"You're a corporate raider," she accused softly, frowning.

"Sometimes," he conceded, "and sometimes a savior, sometimes a venture capitalist. Other times a simple banker, whatever the circumstance requires." He shrugged again. "I was invited into this situation, as it happens."

"Does it happen that way often?" For some reason the answer seemed important.

"Yes. Though sometimes I suspect it's rather like inviting the fox into the hen house."

"I'm sure it is," she muttered, realizing that real money had to be involved here.

He laughed, completely unrepentant.

"What?"

"That's a very sexy drawl you have there."

Flattered despite her better judgment, she replied, "I'm not the only one with an accent."

He grinned at her. "I'm afraid in that you hear my mother who is Greek in every sense of the word."

"And your father?"

"American, of course, born and reared in San Francisco. He died when I was twenty-two. My own childhood was divided neatly between California and Greece."

Interesting. "What's it like there?"

"San Francisco or Greece?"

"Both."

He looked down at her. "Each is close to the ocean, and in many ways defined by it, but San Francisco is soft and green, unlike Greece, which is hard and golden. In my mind, they are opposite sides of the same coin."

She shook her head, enthralled by the poetic manner in which he often spoke. "You're an odd man."

"Perhaps. I like to experience a moment fully."

"Some things you can't know fully."

"And those are the best things," he said, leaning close. "Consider. The things that are easy to know are fleeting, but those which engage and hold us, that is the stuff of life. No?''

She thought for a moment, then decided that she didn't want to think. If she thought too much, she would think of a reason to push him away, and he was too entertaining, too interesting. Besides, once this flight landed and they went their separate ways, she would undoubtedly never see him again. What harm could come of enjoying his company now? Relaxing somewhat she teased, ''You're a philosopher, too, I think.''

He grinned. ''Of course. I am half Greek, after all.''

''Genetics.''

''Always. Everything living is about genetics, everything human, certainly. Especially sex.'' She blinked at him, and found herself snared, suspended in an instant of frighteningly delicious awareness. Then he smiled and added, ''Don't you agree?''

She couldn't breathe, let alone form cogent arguments, and she burned from the inside out with a sensual perception that frankly embarrassed her. After a moment, he chuckled lightly, crossed his legs and lifted a hand, pressing his thumb and first two fingers together for emphasis.

''Consider. My aunt Chloe makes the finest baklava in the world. It's not a secret. She'll give the recipe to a stranger passing on the street. She'll take you into her kitchen and walk you through it step by step.'' He lifted his forefinger. ''But hers will be better than yours.'' He spread his hands and shrugged. ''Genetics. It's a gift she inherited from her mother, and, alas, one she will take to her grave, for she has only sons, and like their father they can barely feed themselves. Good men, you understand, but not cooks."

Avis laughed. He was so very entertaining. "And you, I take it, did not inherit the baklava gene?"

"Of a sort." He slapped his flat middle, proclaiming, "I am genetically predisposed to eat as much of Aunt Chloe's baklava as I can before it's too late."

It was a bald-faced lie. He was as fit as an athlete, toned, tanned, muscled, but she was laughing too hard to reprove him, delighted when she should have been wary. Charmed. So much so that when he casually asked a few minutes later where she would be staying in London, she told him as easily as he made her smile. He looked pleased.

"Truly? I am as well."

A horribly thrilling suspicion swept through her. "You aren't. Really?"

"I am," he said. "I am staying in the very same hotel."

"My goodness." She felt the width of her own smile with weak dismay.

He reached across the aisle and helped himself to a small pillow from the seat. "I think we should both get some rest. It will be morning when we arrive."

She nodded and sank back into the corner of her seat. Reaching up, he turned off the small light which they had been sharing and let his seat back. Avis closed her eyes. Was he pursuing her? She had been pursued before, of course, and had been helplessly flattered, but this…this felt so much more dangerous. What a terrifying thought that was!

But she was being foolish. The man lived in California, for pity's sake. Even if she saw him again what difference would it make in the long run? She willed herself to relax and soon felt herself drifting toward sleep, but one thought stayed with her even as she sank into sleep. Lucien Tyrone was staying at the very same hotel as she. What that might mean she dared not consider, even in those unguarded moments of slumber.

The stewardesses wheeled out breakfast. Lucien kept his seat next to Avis. He had not slept beyond snatches that were inevitably interrupted by wildly erotic dreams and the natural result. Avis had managed a couple hours rest, though. He had watched her for a time, wondering what it was about her that so compelled him. She woke looking slightly rumpled and a little confused, but the confusion dissolved almost instantly into a smile. A quick bout with the hairbrush and a touch of lipstick left her as polished as before.

She ate everything on her breakfast plate except the bacon, starting with the fruit. He noted that she took her toast dry and her coffee with a drop of cream. He passed his melon to her, but she only nibbled at it, comfortably quiet. When he'd eaten his fill, he reached into his case for an electric razor and toothbrush, then excused himself to visit the minuscule lavatory.

"Won't be long now," he assured her, resuming

his seat beside her. She smiled, and he resisted the urge to tell her how very beautiful she was.

The stewardess had passed out declaration cards while he was out of his seat, and Avis held hers up, asking, "What do I do with this?"

"Forget it," he said. "It's for those returning to London. You'll get another when you go home. All they really want to know is how much you spend."

"I see. Wouldn't it make more sense to hand them out just to those who need them?"

He smiled. The things were no doubt printed hundreds to the penny. "Maybe someone should suggest that to the customs department."

She caught the light condescension and flicked the flimsy card at him good-naturedly. He laughed, feeling energized. They shared a monitor to watch a day-old news report, which closed with the current exchange rates. A troubled expression clouded her eyes.

"I didn't think to change money before I left."

He reached into his suit coat for his wallet. "I'd be glad to—"

"No," she said, and the soft implacability of it stilled his hand. "No, thank you."

So, there was steel beneath all that soft femininity. Oddly pleased but also a little amused, he said, "I'll just show you where to make the exchange then. There are kiosks at the airport."

She smiled and nodded, then rose to take her turn in the rest room. As she was returning to her seat, the pilot announced their approach, and the seat belt sign dinged on. Luc rose until she was seated, then sat back down in the seat beside her and made ready for their arrival. Glancing in her direction, he noticed the white knuckles curved around the end of her chair arm. Covering her hand with his, he studied her with some concern, but he found only excitement.

"You can't understand," she told him. "You've traveled your whole life, but this is a grand adventure for me, much more than I ever expected really, and the great shame of it is, I'm here because I'm running away from someone." She looked chagrined at that.

It would be, of course, a man. He gripped her hand a little tighter, prepared to marshal his considerable resources. "Who?"

"My stepson."

He almost recoiled, inexplicably shocked. "You don't care for children?"

"Of course, I do. But Ellis isn't a child. He's thirty."

"Thirty?" Luc blurted. "Your *stepson* is thirty years old?"

"My husband was a lot older than me."

He lifted an eyebrow. "It's not often that the spouse is younger than even the stepchild."

"Oh, but I'm older," she confided, adding shyly, "Just by two years."

He would have guessed her to be about twenty-eight, but thirty-two was fine. "I'm thirty-six myself." As if it ought to matter.

Yet, it must have, for she smiled brightly and confided, "I knew you were young."

Young. He'd have called himself mature, experienced. Maybe even a little jaded. When had he stopped thinking of himself as young?

The engines geared down, and suddenly her hand turned beneath his. She gripped him tightly, palm to palm, and caught her breath as the aircraft started its final descent. He grinned, not so jaded, after all, and rode the fine blade of delight all the way to the ground.

Avis felt her stomach flip as the wheels touched down, but the jolt of contact was surprisingly minimal. The whole thing seemed rather anticlimactic, until the engines abruptly throttled down and she found herself thrown back against her seat, the enormous aircraft hurtling down the runway. Then, suddenly, they were sitting on the tarmac at Gatwick Airport, rain spattering softly against the window.

Luc rose before the seat belt sign went off and began gathering their things. The stewardess showed up with a tan trench coat for him. He immediately requested Avis's wrap as well. Avis ducked her head as the stewardess flashed her an irritated look and hurried away. Luc donned his coat, passed her briefcase to her and escorted her to the exit ahead of everyone else. The stewardess appeared with her cloak, which he draped over her shoulders, pulling up the hood to shield her against the lightly spattering rain.

Steps had been rolled up to the plane, and they descended them quickly. At the bottom, they were whisked into a van, along with their luggage and driven toward the terminal. Avis stared through her window at the rain.

"Tomorrow should be warm and sunny," Luc told her, "at least in the afternoon. Or so the weather reports said before I left California."

"Good for sightseeing, then."

"Just be sure to keep an umbrella handy. It is London, after all."

Smiling, she breathed in deeply and purred, "London." She couldn't quite believe she was here. He flashed a look across her face, his gaze coming to rest briefly on her mouth, then he abruptly looked away.

"A porter will be waiting at the gate for our bags," he said. "We'll follow him or her to customs. Just a formality. Is your passport handy?"

"Yes."

"You'll want to exchange some money. Afterward, I'll get you into a cab."

"A cab? I was told I'd have to take a train first." Gatwick was, in fact, a good distance from the city.

He smiled blandly. "Not this trip. The cab will take you to the hotel. It's a little slower, but you won't have to get yourself from Victoria Station to Kensington this way."

She nodded, perplexed. Apparently they wouldn't be sharing transportation to the hotel. Perhaps he had other business to attend first. She dared not ask.

Fixing her attention on her surroundings, she determined to focus on her adventure, not the dangerously attractive man beside her. Lucien Tyrone was no part of her plans, after all. It would undoubtedly be best if they did not bump into one another again on this trip.

Still, she knew, deep down inside where her most private fears and sharpest guilt lay buried, that she would be terribly disappointed if they did not. Which was all the more reason to avoid him.

Glancing at the sky, she found it dreary and gray.

Chapter Three

Avis felt much relieved when Lucien Tyrone handed her down into a clean, comfortable cab some forty or so minutes after they had landed, closed the door with a smile, waved through the window and calmly walked away. At least that's what she told herself. Determined not to think of him, she avidly observed the landscape as she rode in the back of the modern taxi.

The roads were narrow and, it seemed, a little overgrown, but traffic moved quickly, even without the breakneck speeds that made her so nervous in the pavement-rich Dallas/Fort Worth area. Houses and shops stood close together in crazy rows that zigged and zagged without any seeming rhyme or reason, and though never truly pastoral, the setting gradually became more and more congested. She noticed one particular oddity from the beginning. The buildings all seemed to be constructed of several different types and colors of brick. Eventually, she found that she had to ask the driver about it.

"Oy, well now, on account 'er the war. With all the damage of the Blitz, they didn't have time to match brick, did they?"

Oh. The damage done by the German military during the Second World War. Of course. "I see. Thank you very much."

He nodded, a balding, somewhat beefy man, thirty or forty years old, dressed in a T-shirt and slacks. "First time?" he asked jovially. His accent added vowels to all of his words so that it came out sounding like *foist toim.*

She had to smile. "In London? Yes."

"Business, is it?"

She shook her head. "As a matter of fact, I'm on vacation."

"Where you from?"

"Texas."

"Oy, I might 'er guessed. Me sister's a nurse in Houston."

So it went, until the car pulled up in front of the surprisingly modern hotel tucked into a corner off a street lined with a mixture of businesses and residences housed in what had once been rows of very expensive homes. Somehow, the buildings had managed to retain their dignity. The chatty driver turned, hooking an elbow over the back of his seat.

"I hope you enjoy yourself in the city."

"Thank you. I'm sure I will. What do I owe you?"

"Nothing, Miss. The bloke, that gent back at the airport, he took care of it."

"Oh." The door opened at her elbow just then. "Well, thank you again."

"My pleasure, Miss."

She slid out of the vehicle and stood to smile at the uniformed doorman.

"Registration is to your left," he told her, moving quickly to hold open the heavy glass portal to the lobby. "We'll take care of your luggage."

She felt an instant of disappointment in his cultured accent, which was far less colorful than the cabby's, but which turned out to be the norm. "Thank you." Avis moved past him into the small, opulent lobby with its dark, rich woods, glossy marble, thick carpets, brass and a profusion of fresh-cut flowers.

Check-in went smoothly, but the room was not yet ready.

"Would you care for tea while you wait?" the female clerk asked solicitously.

"Yes, I think I would."

"Will you be requiring dinner reservations?"

"Ah, I haven't really thought about it."

"If you'd prefer to dine in this evening, I'd recommend a reservation. We have an excellent little restaurant that draws quite a crowd most nights."

"I see." She glanced over her shoulder and through the window to the street bathed in cold, drizzling rain. "I'll be eating out tomorrow," she decided, "so I might as well stay in tonight."

"You can always take room service." The clerk picked up a small brochure explaining the location of the restaurant within the building and its hours of operation. "Most of our guests seem to prefer the restaurant, however. If you so desire, you can make your reservations in person at tea, or I can handle it for you."

"I'll take care of it," Avis said, pocketing the small brochure.

"Just follow the hallway to my left," the clerk said with a nod. "We'll notify you as soon as the room is ready."

"Do you have a map of the local area?"

"Oh, yes, and also a list of businesses you might find of interest." The young woman handed over both, a placid smile on her pretty face. "If you'd like some reference material on the greater London attractions, you can see the concierge, who will also be happy to make any bookings you might require."

Avis nodded. "Thank you."

She stopped by the concierge's desk and picked up several brochures from him before following the hall to the restaurant, which sat across the way from the closed bar with its heavy brass and gleaming ebony fixtures. Her complementary tea came with cheese toast and a platter of fruit, all served cheerfully but unobtrusively from an ornate silver trolley in the small but equally opulent dining room. Sitting at a table dressed with a crisp white cloth and fresh flowers before a cheery fire in the marble-faced hearth while sipping a cup of strong, milky tea, the reality of her situation settled over her at last.

She was in England. London and all its treasures lay waiting for her beyond this safe, warm, comfortable place. And somewhere nearby was Lucien Tyrone. She shivered, but whether with anticipation or distress she honestly couldn't say.

She had ventured out on her own, well bundled against the continuing drizzle, down the street and around the corner to the chemist's, according to the concierge. Luc approved and, in truth, had expected nothing less. She had journeyed all the way to London on her own, after all. He would be surprised, even disappointed, if she had then hidden away timidly inside this comfortable little hotel. Besides, it suited his purposes to have her safely out of the way when he finally checked in.

Though he had asked his friend to warn the staff that he wanted to keep a low profile, a direct call from the chairman of the board of governors of the hotel's parent company was bound to set off some alarms with the staff, and seeing him being greeted rather obsequiously by the manager of the hotel himself would undoubtedly have made Avis think.

Though she might not come to the conclusion that he was shunning a very fine townhouse, much to his housekeeper's dismay, in order to set himself up near her in a small hotel suite. She almost certainly would have realized that his plans had been made very last-minute, say on the drive in from the airport in his chauffeured limousine, which was why he'd thought it best to send her along by herself in a cab.

He wasn't going to take any chances on derailing his campaign. Oh, it wasn't as if he had lied to her, not technically, anyway. He just didn't think it wise to tell her more of the truth than she needed to know at this time.

On the other hand, Lucien Tyrone never considered whether or not he was due whatever information he deemed necessary to his cause and neither, apparently, did those of whom he sought intelligence, so he hadn't thought twice about asking for Avis's room number, where she had gone and what plans she might have made. The hotel staff apparently hadn't thought twice about telling him whatever he wanted to know, so he didn't hesitate to have himself a place added to her dinner table. He did, however, try to make their meeting in the dining room look somewhat unexpected.

"Well, hello again. Mind if I join you? Or are you expecting someone else?"

For a moment she merely stared up at him from her burgundy leather club chair, her wide eyes a heady blue, thanks in part to the long-sleeved, cunningly simple dress that she wore. Made of a slinky knit fabric of red-violet, it clung to her delicious curves with loving detail and yet remained surprisingly modest, despite a soft neckline that puddled inviting over her impressive cleavage and called attention to the elegant V of her collarbone. A man could slide his hands inside that top and reach just about anything he wanted. Luc leaned forward slightly, making her a gentle bow and letting the hang of his suit jacket and tie camouflage a certain disturbing development below his waist.

"Feel free," she said, sweeping a graceful hand at

the empty chair to her left, where a setting of china awaited him.

Satisfied, he took the seat and absently received the menu offered by the servant hovering at his shoulder. "Any suggestions?" he asked of her.

"I usually just go for the special," she confessed. "The waiter said it's commonly called 'Jenny in snow' or something like that."

He snapped his menu closed and nodded at the waiter. "Ah, yes. A lovely hunk of beef slow-roasted in a potato and salt crust. Not so good for the blood pressure, I'm sure, but a delight on the tongue. Perhaps we'd better order a good red wine to help the digestion." She rolled her eyes, smiling. "You may scoff," he told her with a mock frown, "but the Europeans swear by it."

"They do seem to have a lower incidence of cholesterol and heart disease than we Americans," she conceded wryly.

"Speak for yourself," he quipped. "I've enough healthy Mediterranean blood pumping through these veins to eat as I choose." He swept his gaze over her and added softly, "Then again, you look the very picture of health yourself. A beautiful thing. To be healthy."

She dropped her gaze, a demure blush rising to her cheeks, and he silently congratulated himself on hitting just the right note. He picked the wine, unimpressed by the selection.

Early on, conversation revolved around her drive into the city. He expressed regret for not having been able to offer her a ride into town but didn't explain why that had been the case. When he casually mentioned that he had gotten more done that afternoon than expected and so would have the next day free, she naturally assumed that his endeavors had involved business, which they had, at least so far as rearranging his schedule. Now to arrange hers.

"Have you planned your conquest?"

"Conquest?"

"I expect you'll take the city by storm," he teased, "but with so much to see and do, one must plan. Oh, but your escort will have laid down a route for you, I suppose."

"Escort?"

Her obvious confusion put to rest any doubts he might have had about the possibility of her meeting someone here, but he wisely didn't let on. "Yes, is he local? Or perhaps the person you're meeting is a she?"

Avis blinked at him, and the sultry movement of those smooth eyelids did wildly erotic things to his insides. Then her blush rose again. "Oh. Ah." He smiled, too charmed by her embarrassment to let her off the hook. "That was only...actually, I only meant that I intended to engage a tour guide."

He contrived surprise and tried to keep the delight under wraps. "Well, in that case, you must let me be your tour guide."

Her chest heaved as she surreptitiously caught her breath, lifting that lovely bosom so high that his mouth began to water. "I–I don't want to impose."

"Nonsense. You'd be doing me a favor, actually. Despite today's progress, my business is not going to proceed as quickly as I'd planned. You know how it is. I'm afraid I'm going to have lots of time on my hands this trip, and once you've seen the sights, the only way to really enjoy them again is to show them to someone who hasn't.'' A veritable parade of emotions made its way across her face, delaying her answer long enough for him to add a heartfelt, ''Please. I can guarantee you all the highlights and some secrets you'll miss otherwise.'' How true. How very true.

She gave in with some trepidation. ''Well, I wouldn't want to monopolize all your free time.''

''We can play it by ear,'' he assured her, ''but I am available tomorrow.''

She let out a tense breath and laughed a little. ''All right, if you're sure.''

''Positive.'' He smiled and decided to push a bit. ''If you have no plans for later this evening, perhaps you'd like to come out to the theater with me. The production has been running for a while, so I'm sure there are tickets to be had.'' He had them, in fact, in reserve, a box for the whole season. He hadn't even intended to use them tonight, which was just as well since she shook her head firmly.

''I really need to get some rest tonight if I'm going to get the most out of tomorrow.''

Oh, well, nothing ventured, nothing gained. ''You didn't nap this afternoon then. Very good. It's always best to hold out, get on the local schedule right away.''

She nodded. ''I've heard that's how to beat the jet lag.''

They talked about that and other things to do with travel until their dinners arrived. And then they moved onto the next day's agenda. He steered her away from governmental buildings and royal establishments where he might be able to arrange private tours for her later. The museums she could manage safely on her own while he had to tend to business, since he couldn't put off everything entirely, but he didn't tell her that. With some prodding on his part, they finally settled on the obvious, the colossal Ferris wheel known as the London Eye, the replicated Globe Theatre, with London Bridge thrown in if time allowed, and of course, the Tower of London. Some of these were among the more "touristy" of London's offerings, in his opinion, but should not be missed, nonetheless.

"I know a wonderful little place overlooking the Thames where we can have lunch, if you like," he suggested hopefully.

"Sounds perfect."

He grinned. "What a lucky thing that we met. I'd have been bored to tears otherwise."

She gave him another of those reticent smiles, part pure shyness, part reluctance and suspicion. His mind worked furiously to find a way to eliminate the latter, but before he could properly apply himself to the problem, a hearty voice assaulted his ear.

"Hello! It's Tyrone himself. How are you buddy boy? Slumming a bit are we? Good to see you. Imagine bumping into you this way. And who is this beauty?"

As usual, Colbert barely drew breath between

questions and statements, let alone wait for reply. Luc
jovially accepted the inevitable and rose to greet his
old chum.

Col was a bluff, good-natured fellow with a rapidly
receding hairline and a waist that seemed determined
to make up the difference. The two had "racketed
around town" together at one time, to use Colbert's
parlance. Col's marriage had put an end to that, but
they dashed off notes to one another from time to
time, though actually getting together always seemed
impossible especially since Althea's death. Luc suspected that most of the responsibility lay with Lady
Colbert, who seemed to fear that a single Lucien
would lead her husband into pursuits designed to
threaten their carefully guarded wedded bliss.

After rising to accept Col's back pounding and delivering his own greeting in kind, Luc made the in-
troduction. "Allow me to present Mrs. Avis Lorimer.
Avis, you've the dubious honor of meeting Sir Ponder
Colbert, London Minister of…what is it again, Col?"

"Fiduciary Disbursement of Avenue," Col announced importantly, then clarified, "my office doles
out the funds for street repair in this old burg. How
do you do, Mrs. Lorimer."

"Fine, thank you. And yourself?"

He waved a pudgy hand self-importantly. "Busy.
Busy day and night."

"I can believe that, considering how much road
work I encountered on my drive through the city this
morning."

Col made a face. "Barriers only, most likely.
That's the trouble with the system. Contractors get

first payments the instant the barriers go up, so they rush out and set up traffic cones, even block off entire streets, before the ink dries on the contracts, then it's months before the real work begins. Filthy nuisance, but can I get it changed? Not on your life." He turned instantly to Luc again. "Gad, it's good to see you, even if you do look ten years younger than me."

"Excuse me," Avis said, quickly rising to her feet. "I'm exhausted, so if you don't mind I'll just leave you two gentlemen to visit."

"No need to rush off on my account," Col assured her.

"I'm ready to call it a night, frankly. Been a long day. Nice meeting you."

Col bobbed a quick bow. "A pleasure."

Before she could get off, Luc captured her hand. Leaning in to kiss her cheek, he softly inquired, "Is eight too early to meet down here for breakfast?"

"That's fine," she replied, smiling even as she pulled away. He watched her walk out of the restaurant, marveling at how that dress so fluidly delineated her curves. She would be glorious naked.

At his elbow, Col rocked back on his heels and cleared his throat. "And Mr. Lorimer would be where?"

Luc slid him a sideways glare. "Dead and buried for some years now."

Col grinned. "Still the same old Luc. Trust you to come up with the most delectable widow on two continents. No doubt the bed she's about to climb into is yours."

"Not tonight," Luc said easily, reseating himself.

He leaned forward as Col pulled out a chair of his own and added confidently, "But tomorrow night will be a different story."

"Cocky," Col pronounced, signaling the waiter. "Now tell me what evil you've been up to while I get a drink and cancel my meeting."

Avis paced the room in her bare feet for some time before coming to a decision firm enough to allow her the rest she so desperately needed. She had no illusions about Lucien Tyrone's intentions. Kenneth had destroyed any silly trust she might have had in a man's friendship long ago, which was also the last time she had been so ardently, systematically pursued. Lucien wanted sex, a brief, torrid affair to relieve the tedium of business travel. In the long run, she supposed his goal was less harmful than Kenneth's had been.

Oh, he, too, had been after the hot and sweaty release of sex, but more than that he'd wanted someone pleasant whom he could manipulate, someone to make his life comfortable and easy. She'd been just gullible and emotionally destitute enough to fall into his trap.

The gullibility no longer existed, but to her dismay, her own desires remained. She had known from the moment she'd sat down at the dinner table for whom that extra place setting had been laid, but instead of telling the waiter that a mistake had been made, she'd sat there like an idiot just waiting for him to put in his appearance. And that dress. A simple skirt and blouse would have sufficed, but she'd worn something designed to make him take notice, and it had worked. Better than she'd hoped.

She plopped down on the foot of her bed, which was surprisingly firm, and admitted to herself a difficult truth. All right, so she wanted to be found lovely and desirable by a lovely and desirable man. It was only natural. She was a woman, after all, and no one understood the dangers better than she did.

She had tried so hard over the years not to think that she had allowed, no, helped, Kenneth ruin her life, but the fact was that almost from the beginning she had felt trapped and miserably unhappy in her marriage. She was determined not to let anything similar occur again. Why was she having difficulty convincing herself that it would in this case?

She pondered that for a moment and came to the conclusion that this trip was a moment out of time, a complete departure from her daily life. Once she and Lucien Tyrone parted ways, that would be the end of it. She would return to her life, and he would return to his. They lived half a continent apart, for heaven's sake, and if nothing else, his work would keep him far away from her. Surely she could afford to let down her guard for a few days. He was so very entertaining. Seeing London with him would be a once-in-a-lifetime treat. It didn't have to be more than that. She could always walk away if it got too complicated.

Just knowing that she had devised a convenient justification for herself, she felt better. Sliding down into the quite firm bed, she took a last look around her before shutting off the light. The room was on the small side, but the furnishings were elegant and traditional, with gleaming rosewoods and cool, restful greens to recommend them. The landscapes on the wall were tastefully done, the flowered draperies decorative without being ornate. A pair of wingback chairs and a side table had been placed in front of the smallest fireplace she had ever seen. An electrical unit had been installed inside the fireplace, so she was not to have the luxury of a real fire, but the red glow of the now-cooling unit lent a cheery ambience to the room. She was content for the moment. Tomorrow would bring its own adventures, but for tonight, rest was all she wanted.

Switching off the light, she snuggled into downy pillows that made up somewhat for the hard mattress and let herself drift away.

Chapter Four

She skipped. She couldn't help it. There inside the imposing gray walls of the old fortress known as the Tower of London, sunshine warming the soft spring air and verdant green beneath her feet, surrounded by historical significance and unbelievable treasure, with a laughing, indulgent man at her side, what else was a woman on a trip of delightful discovery to do but skip? Luc laughed and let her go, turning with her, his arms outstretched as if to catch her should she stumble, while she skipped in circles around him.

Breathless, she finally collapsed on a bench, pulling him along with her. "My feet are killing me!" She didn't quite mean that; she was still full of the wonder of the day.

Lucien grinned and snaked an arm about her waist, pulling her over onto one hip and around to face him.

He'd been doing that all day, touching her with casual purpose, as if he had a right to or, more accurately, as if serving her notice that he was claiming the right to touch her in any fashion he chose.

"I never knew being a tourist could be such fun," he told her huskily.

She smiled, feeling the now-familiar sizzle of electricity. "Me neither, but it has been fun, hasn't it?"

"Very much."

She allowed herself to relax and placed a hand on his shoulder. "What's been your favorite part?"

"The Eye."

She wrinkled her nose. "Too crowded."

"Ah, but the view was spectacular, more so because I was plastered against you."

She no longer blinked or blushed at such flirtations from him. His many compliments and innuendoes had started a slow heat in the pit of her belly that had warmed her thoroughly this whole day. "So naughty," she scolded teasingly.

He nodded, a smile lurking at one corner of his mouth. Pure desire burned behind those charcoal eyes, and it touched off sparks of the same in her.

Suddenly he rose, snagging her hand on the way up. "Come. Time to get those poor feet of yours back to the hotel for a nice soak."

"Mmm." She closed her eyes and let him pull her onto those aching feet. "You have such lovely ideas."

"Here's another," he said, sliding his arm around her waist as they walked toward the exit. "Let me take you to dinner tonight. I know a grand restaurant near the Royal Albert, very formal, very stuffy, very good. I'll give you time to rest and dress properly.''

''Hmm, it could be fun to dress up.''

''You could always wear that scrumptious thing you wore last night. It really deserves a wider audience.''

She laughed. ''Thank you, but I do have another I've been saving for a special occasion.''

He drew her a little tighter against him. ''Do you? That's definitely something to look forward to, then. How is about half–past eight?''

''Perfect, but are you sure you can get reservations?''

He just smiled and led her away from the river to the street, where he quickly hailed one of those famous black cabs with the wide doors and high seats. On the ride back to the hotel, he insisted on pulling off her shoes and rubbing her stockinged feet. Her embarrassment didn't last long against his talented hands; she felt like butter by the time they arrived. While he paid the cabby, she hastily began donning her shoes again, but he took them from her, declaring, ''No need.''

Then he swung her up into his arms as she stepped out of the vehicle and carried her easily across the chilly pavement and through the door to the hotel lobby, where he deposited her as casually as if he toted around shoeless women every day.

She managed a breathless, ''Thank you.'' He inclined his head and looked down at her with those steamy eyes of his. Her heartbeat accelerated. ''I-I'll see you later.''

"Umm," he said, handing over her shoes, "but you'll kiss me now." His tone implied that he had waited quite long enough, and something in her agreed with him, for she just stood there in the hotel lobby, clutching her worn loafers to her chest, while he stepped closer, delicately touched her face with the fingertips of both hands and bowed his head to meet her mouth with his.

That's all it was, a meeting of the mouths, eyes closed, bodies yearning but not touching. For a long, sweet moment, their lips formed softly against one another, and then a tremor shook him, a deeply internal quake that telegraphed itself through his fingertips and the merest touch that he maintained along the ridges of her cheekbones. Immediately, he dropped his hands and lifted his head. The look in his eyes poured over her like hot lava. Scalded, she backed away, then whirled and walked swiftly toward the elevators on stockinged feet.

As she moved, she became aware of her surroundings again and how busily everyone else was attending his or her own business. The elevator doors slid closed in front of her burning face, but as she rose upward, the heat that rode with her had nothing at all to do with embarrassment and everything to do with losing her mind.

The proof of that came nearly two hours later. The light knock fell upon her door while she was still in her bathrobe, just having finished her face and pinned up her hair. Her elegant, sapphire dress lay spread out across the bed. It was early yet, but she knew instantly who it would be. She did not, however, expect to find him standing there in tuxedo pants and pin-tucked shirt, without a jacket, two stemmed glasses in one hand and a wine bottle in the other. His smile seemed perfunctory and troubled. He spoke without preamble.

"I know I'm rushing you, but I find that I simply cannot sit through a long public dinner without embarrassing myself."

"Whyever not? What's wrong?"

"What's wrong?" He bowed his head, looking up at her from beneath the smooth jut of his brow. "Nothing is *wrong,* but I find that I cannot stop thinking about making love to you, and that presents a certain…condition not acceptable in public."

His firm, silky tone, the heat in his eyes, each alone was enough to undo any resolve she might have knotted together since that kiss in the hotel lobby. She gulped, knowing what would happen if she let him cross her threshold.

"You'd better come in."

Standing back, she cleared the doorway, then closed it after he strolled through, the tense line of his shoulders at odds with his easy amble. He looked around him for someplace to put the wine and glasses. Finding the table, he moved to it and carefully situated each item before turning to the bed. He picked up the dress by the shoulders and studied it as if picturing exactly how it would look on her.

"You have exquisite taste," he told her.

She stood before the electric fire and folded her hands to disguise their trembling. "Thank you."

He draped the dress over one of the chairs and

finally looked at her, his intention blatant. "My room is larger," he said huskily. "We can go there if you like." It was too stupid an idea to even entertain, so she just looked at him. Suddenly he stepped close and pulled her into his arms, running his hands over her back and bottom with proprietary command. He sighed, his chin resting in her hair and whispered, "You know how beautiful you are, don't you?"

"Yes," she answered, and it was true. In that moment out of time, she was the most beautiful woman in the world, and she knew that she would never forget it.

"I feel as if I've waited my entire life to make love to you," he said, and that was how he did it, as if touching her, kissing her, laying her bare and exploring her body with tender adoration were somehow the culmination of a lifetime of desire and planning, a hard-won goal meant to be savored and relished, wrung of every last drop of pleasure.

But if it was all that for him, it was nothing more nor less than total surprise for her, one gasping, glorious discovery after another. She had never understood what sex could be like with a young, virile man, gentle and hard, lazy and rushed, intense and serene all at once. She had not expected the beauty of it or the wonder, let alone the intense, prolonged orgasms that left her sated and hungry at the same time. She felt like a fool at times and worldly-wise at the end and, finally, knew that she would never blush again.

Luc lay back against the pillows, one arm curled above his head, the other holding her lush form against his side. The pins had fallen from her silky hair, and it fanned across his chest, a living blanket of waves and large, tumbling curls. He felt oddly triumphant and amazingly replete. And puzzled.

Her little gasps of surprise and pleasure still echoed inside him. The dainty, tentative brush of her hands still swept his flesh with sensual memory. The way she had arched her back and wrapped her legs around him felt, even now, oddly poignant. Neither of them could deny that the sex had been extraordinarily fulfilling, and yet something was missing, something upon which he couldn't quite put his finger.

It wasn't as if she had held back, and yet he sensed that he had merely peeked beneath her surface tonight. He had realized upon their meeting that her serene facade masked a highly sensual nature, but now he was beginning to understand how deeply passionate and, yes, even volatile, that sensuality was. Clearly, he had yet to plumb those depths, and he very much wanted to, perhaps even *needed* to. He didn't like that, didn't like it at all.

Still, he could be a pragmatic man. He had what he had. He could only deal with it as it was. And one night, or two or three, wasn't going to give him enough time for the task. He decided that he was going to close the gate on her, keep her close at hand. At least until he settled this thing in his own mind. What he had told her before was entirely too true. He always wanted to *know* things, and Avis Lorimer compelled him in a way no other woman ever had. He silently vowed that he would solve the mystery of her before he was done.

Clearing his throat, he asked, "Are you hungry?"

She didn't answer for a moment, as if she was taking stock. "Yes."

He reached across the bed, lifted the telephone receiver from its cradle and punched a button. "This is Mr. Tyrone," he said to whoever answered the ring. "Could you connect me with Room Service please? Thank you." He lowered the receiver and spoke to Avis. "Have a taste for anything in particular?"

"Not really."

He went back to the telephone. "Mr. Tyrone here. I realize your kitchen is probably closed, but we haven't eaten this evening. What could you send up? Chateaubriand?" He looked down at Avis and lifted an eyebrow. She shrugged. "That's fine then."

"And something sweet," she said.

"And dessert," he said into the phone, still querying her with his eyes.

"Chocolate," she decided.

"Any chocolate taking up space down there? Pudding? Pudding is excellent. And I think that's it." He gave the person on the other end of the line the room number and hung up.

Avis rolled over and propped her chin on his chest, looking tousled and sleepy and sated. "Do you always get what you want when you want it?"

"Usually," he admitted, "but I can be a surprisingly patient man."

"I admire patience," she said. "I have to work at it myself."

He studied her for a moment. "You're a puzzling woman."

She sat up, carrying the covers with her, leaving only her lovely shoulders and arms bare. "What makes you say that?"

"Well, for one thing, you somehow seem a very patient sort to me."

She shook her head. "No, not really. I mean, I learned to be, but it was a struggle, and I know now that I couldn't be that patient again."

He tilted his head. "And what does that mean, *again?*"

She just looked at him. "Once I was patient, for a long time, but I don't think I could be again. That's all."

Seeing that she was not going to say anything else, he sighed. "Definitely a puzzle." He reached up to tap her chest with a finger. "I sense secrets in there."

She tilted her head. "Is that what interests you? Ferreting out my secrets?"

"About as much as this," he said, pulling the covers out of her grasp, revealing the most naturally perfect breasts he'd ever seen.

She sat there staring down at him, her rich blue eyes brushing his with their gaze. Then she abruptly flopped down on top of him and wrapped her arms around his neck. "I'll never tell," she whispered tauntingly.

He laughed and flipped her over, yanking back the covers completely. "Yes, you will."

She shook her head. "And you can't make me."

"Famous last words," he promised, on his knees. He ran his hands from her collarbone to her thighs, rollicking in every sumptuous hill and gentle valley along the way. When dinner came, he yelled for them to leave it outside the door. It was much later, after a tepid meal and full bottle of good wine, that he discovered to his surprise that neither sex nor food had diminished his appetite for dessert.

Chocolate pudding would ever after be his favorite.

The sun was glaring when the warm body next to her stretched and groaned. On her stomach, Avis pushed hair out of her eyes and managed to lift her head. "Morning."

The man who grinned at her was in sore need of a shave and looked more stunning than ever with his hair going every which way and his eyes heavy with sleep. "Good morning, beautiful." He smoothed her hair with one hand and groaned again. "This bed is awfully hard."

"I noticed that the first night."

He burrowed beneath the covers and pulled her up onto his chest. "But not last night, hmm?"

One corner of her mouth kicked up. "Can't say that I did."

He kissed her with full attention, then broke off. "What time is it anyway?"

"Haven't a clue."

He fumbled around for his watch and lifted it from the bedside table. "Damn, I've missed a meeting. Lofton is probably pulling out his hair." He'd intentionally left his cell phone in his own room so he couldn't be reached, but he hadn't expected to spend the whole night here or to sleep so late. "Well, to hell with it," he decided aloud. "I own the damned company. I can blow a deal if I want."

"Oh, no," Avis worried aloud. "You didn't really?"

He grinned at her. "Probably not. But so what if I did?"

Avis bit her lip, weighing the wisdom of her own curiosity. "Can I ask you something?"

"Of course."

"How rich are you?"

He didn't blink an eye. "Very. Why?"

She frowned. "Just lots of little things have made me wonder."

"Does it matter?"

"I suppose not. I'm quite comfortable myself."

"I know."

"You do?"

"Don't be offended," he cautioned, pushing up onto his elbows, "but I had you checked out. That's not very romantic, but I'm afraid it's pretty much a necessity in my case."

Her frown deepened. "*That* rich?"

He nodded. "I have another confession to make."

"And that is?"

He rubbed one eyebrow. "I only stayed in this hotel to be near you."

As if that was news. "I know."

"I actually own quite a spacious house here in town."

She sat up, stunned, but not so shocked that she didn't remember to pull the pillow into her lap to cover herself. "A house?"

"Nearby, actually."

"Well, why didn't you just say so?"

"I was afraid that if I gave you too much space you'd put up a wall, and I didn't want to spend all our time together tearing it down again."

All our time. A finite thing. Just moments removed from reality. She would soon be leaving this man behind her as completely as if he had never existed, which raised another question. "Why are you telling me this now?"

He sat up, looped an arm about her shoulders. "Stay with me. Come home with me. Give us this time together here in London." She sighed, and he pressed. "Please. You know you want to. We'll have such fun. I'll make it magical, I promise."

She couldn't catch the smile that broke across her face. *Magical* was the word for what had taken place last night. "You sound like a little boy pleading for a treat."

"The bed's soft," he whispered against her ear.

"I suppose there's a fireplace in every room, too," she quipped chidingly.

"Even the bath. Right next to the tub, which is huge, by the way."

Her eyes almost crossed as she imagined what magic he could work there.

"We'd have a great deal more privacy," he argued, "and it would be easier for me to take care of business from there. So I could spend more time with you." He wound a finger in a lock of her hair, and she wondered why she was even pretending to dither when she had every intention of agreeing.

"Oh, all right."

It wasn't a particularly gracious capitulation, but he practically whooped with glee. "I'll call the desk and check us both out."

"No! I don't want to check out."

"Why not?"

Because then everyone back home will know that we're having an affair, she thought, but she only said, "Chalk it up to pride if you have to have a reason."

He rolled his eyes. "I suppose that means you won't even let me pay the bill."

She folded her arms around the pillow. "Of course not."

For some reason he laughed and kissed her quickly as he reached for the telephone. "You are special, do you know that? Unique among women, I suspect."

She smiled inside. Outwardly she feared that she glowed, but she quashed it with a simple nod of her head. "I suppose I'd better pack a bag," she said. "Could you take it along to your room when you go?"

"My bags are almost empty," he said with a wry smile. "I never bring much with me since I keep a house here, and most of what I did bring, I left there. So you can use my luggage if you want. We'll pick up yours later."

She nodded and crawled out of the bed, holding the pillow lengthwise in front of her. "Well, what are you waiting for then? Run get the luggage."

He bounded up, still naked. "I suppose you'll have my head if I send a porter back with it."

She let him know with a look how right he was.

Chuckling, he yanked on his pants and shirt while she maneuvered into her robe, juggling that pillow. She got the sash belted just as he stuffed his bare feet into his dress shoes.

"I'll be back as soon as I get cleaned up and make a few phone calls," he told her.

"All right."

He kissed her then and tugged at the end of her sash. "All that fancy footwork wasn't necessary, you know. Your body is stunningly beautiful."

She bowed her head. "Thank you."

"I like that you're modest, actually."

She rolled her eyes at that. She'd have said that modesty had gone out the window the night before. "You're certainly not modest," she said.

"No. Does that bother you?"

"Not really."

"Good." He kissed her again. "We'll have breakfast in the car if that's all right."

She shrugged, a little surprised.

"What would you like? Fresh fruit and pastries all right?"

"Fine."

"And coffee with cream, just enough to muddy it a bit?"

She smiled because he had remembered something so unimportant.

"I'll let the driver know," he told her with a self-satisfied smile of his own.

Driver. Of course. Breakfast in the back of a limo, and not via the local drive-through, should there be such a thing in London. "I'll be ready," she promised, and he kissed her once more before slipping out into the hall.

She turned away from the closed door and caught sight of the rumpled, happy woman in the closet mirror. "One of us has lost her ever-loving mind," she said, but the woman in the mirror didn't seem to care a whit.

They ate breakfast in the back of a cream-colored limousine which was shorter than the American version but sturdier and quite roomy, not that Avis had much experience in that area, about as much experience as she had with vacation affairs, to be exact. She sipped her coffee (with cream) from fine bone china while plucking fruit from crystal and buttering her scone with heavy silver. They were scarcely around the corner, however, before Lucien's cell phone rang.

"Yes, yes," he said. "Within the hour." He folded the tiny phone and stowed it in the inside coat pocket from which he'd taken it.

"I'm sorry. I won't be free until mid-afternoon. I thought we might do Kew Gardens then, but if you like, my driver Baldwin will take you to one of the museums in town. Or maybe you'd prefer to spend the morning shopping? I could—"

"A museum would be lovely," she interrupted before he could offer to pick up her shopping bills.

He nodded, one corner of his mouth curled in a knowing smile. "I would suggest that we try that restaurant I mentioned yesterday, but if I know Mrs. Baldwin, who is my housekeeper and cook, she's already planning this evening's menu, and since I've disappointed her once already this trip, I thought we might dine in tonight.''

Avis nodded, a little disconcerted by the thought of housekeepers and drivers. "Are you sure it's a good idea for me to stay at your place?"

"It's an excellent idea," Luc insisted, squeezing her hand. "I don't want to miss a moment with you."

Avis bit her lip. "You're not embarrassed to be bringing a woman home with you?"

He tilted his head, shifting around in his seat a little to look at her. "Shall I tell you what Mrs. Baldwin said this morning when I called to inform her? She said, 'It's bloody well about time.' She's worried about me, you see, thinks I'm too much alone since my wife died."

Avis lifted an eyebrow. "Are you trying to tell me that I'm the first woman you've been with these past four years?"

He seemed a bit startled. "No. I'm not trying to tell you that."

"I suppose I'm just the first woman you've taken home with you?"

He blinked at her and sat back, folding his arms. After a moment, he reached up to rub his cleanly shaven chin. "Actually, you are." He frowned. "I just realized it."

"Well, that's something," she said softly.

"You don't understand," he said, eyes moving side to side as if he was mentally sifting through a lengthy list. "I have homes all over the world, and I've never taken a woman to any of them before, not since my wife died."

That shouldn't have made her feel special, but somehow it did. She shook her head. "All over the world, huh?"

He shrugged. "Gdansk, Madrid, Buenos Aires, Sydney, Bangkok, Martinique, and Sirinos, um, just outside of Athens."

When she could get her mouth closed again, she mumbled, "Not to mention San Francisco."

"Or Manhattan," he added, nodding.

"Oh, my," Avis said, and he looked up, surprised. "What?"

Her brow furrowed. "That's an awfully broad playing field you've got there. Sort of redefines the term *home,* doesn't it?"

"Not really. I actually dislike hotels, but my business interests keep me traveling. It's nice to have someplace of your own, a base of operations. In my case it's necessary to have many bases."

"You can't be in any one place long enough to actually feel at home, though."

"On the contrary. I've known most of these houses since I was a boy."

She could only shake her head. What had he rattled off, eight or nine "homes?" No, ten. Mustn't forget London.

Toto, she thought, *we aren't in Kansas anymore.* Heck, this wasn't just a moment out of time, it was a whole other world, and one in which she knew she could never belong. Fortunately, she wouldn't have to, at least not for long, but it might be fun to pretend. For a little while.

Chapter Five

Avis needn't have worried about her reception from Luc's household staff. Plump, sixty-something Mrs. Baldwin, with her graying, untidy hair, oddly dressy pantsuit and kind smile, was only too glad to meet her.

"Welcome. Welcome. I hope everything is to your liking."

"Oh, please, don't go to any trouble on my account," Avis told her, standing self-consciously in the high-ceilinged marble foyer of a very fine Kensington row house.

"Don't listen to her," Luc said, kissing the diminutive Mrs. Baldwin on the cheek. "She doesn't know that you live to pamper."

To Avis's surprise, Mrs. Baldwin swatted her employer on the forearm. "And whom would I pamper?'' she demanded. ''You're never home even when you're here.'' She smiled at Avis and clapped her hands together. ''At least it wasn't business keeping you away this time.''

The tall, redheaded young man introduced to Avis as Lofton cleared his throat. She thought she might recognize him from the airplane, but not so much as a flicker of familiarity had ruffled his calm, blandly handsome face. ''Speaking of business...'' he said suggestively.

Mrs. Baldwin frowned, but Lucien clasped Avis's hand, leaning in to kiss her swiftly on the mouth. ''I'm sorry, but I do have to go. When Baldwin returns with the car, you just tell him where you want him to take you, all right? I'll join you as quickly as I can.''

''You can't leave this child on her own,'' Mrs. Baldwin protested.

''It's perfectly all right,'' Avis said quickly. ''I understand.''

''No, no,'' Luc interjected, holding up a hand in surrender. ''I've been properly chastised. How about this, my dear Mrs. Baldwin? I'll engage a guide for our lovely Avis, so that when I can't be with her, she won't be sightseeing on her own.''

''Lucien,'' Avis began, ''that's not nec—''

''Well, I suppose, if it's the best that you can do,'' sniffed Mrs. Baldwin, folding her arms beneath her heavy breasts.

Lucien bowed slightly from the waist. ''Consider it done then.'' He winked at Avis and, followed

swiftly by Lofton, went out, leaving her feeling somewhat overwhelmed.

Mrs. Baldwin beamed at her. "Right then. Now
let's get you settled, love. We've an empty dressing
room that's been waiting far too long for something
feminine." With that, she headed off down a wide
central hall, the same one through which Mr. Baldwin, the chauffeur and a large, dignified, silent man,
had earlier carried Lucien's bags filled with Avis's
things.

Avis followed, her steps slowing as she took in her
surroundings. A number of doors stood open off that
wide central hallway, revealing drawing and dining
rooms that featured plastered walls in a rich shade of
ruddy wine, accented with creamy painted woodwork. The furnishings were quite formal and appeared to be antiques, as did the ornately framed
paintings and colorful area rugs. Mrs. Baldwin busily
explained that some of the walls could be taken down
panel by panel, creating a grand ballroom.

"Of course," she added, "we haven't had a ball
here since Mr. Lucien's wedding."

A library paneled in dark, gleaming wood displayed hundreds of leather-bound volumes, a pair of
enormous desks and a hand-painted globe the size of
a small automobile. The remaining rooms were less
formal. One contained a billiards table and well-
stocked bar, another comfortable, overstuffed furni-
ture and a flat-screen television. The closed doors,
Mrs. Baldwin informed her, were those of the gentlemen's and ladies' retiring rooms, each denoted by a

brass *G* or *L* placed discreetly above the crystal door knobs.

At the back of the house, a second hallway crossed the first. Mrs. Baldwin waved to the left even as she turned right. "You can reach the kitchen, staff quarters and garage that way." She pointed straight ahead and added, "You'll find a hidden staircase just around that corner, and here…" She stopped and opened a door inlaid with heavy brass grillwork. "Mrs. Eugenia had this elevator installed. This used to be a storage room."

Avis gaped. An elevator. In a private home. She shook her head, followed the housekeeper into the roomy compartment and thought to ask, "Who is Mrs. Eugenia?"

"Dear me," exclaimed Mrs. Baldwin, pushing a button, "that would be Lucien's mother. You haven't met her then?" The elevator lifted off.

"Ah…no."

"Just as well," Mrs. Baldwin chirped. An instant later, the elevator stopped and Mrs. Baldwin opened the door.

They stepped out into a small antechamber from which two more bright hallways branched off, a long one to the right and a short one straight ahead. Mrs. Baldwin walked through the latter and threw open double doors, revealing a stunning gold-and-blue sitting room elegantly furnished with white damask chairs and sofas arranged in front of a massive white marble fireplace. The bedchamber, decorated in the same tones of gold and cool blue, was accented with stunning splashes of crimson, including the silk spread on the massive four-poster bed and a waist-high crystal vase overflowing with dozens of fresh roses. The woods were all golden and warm, including those that fronted the fireplace opposite the bed.

Avis stood in the center of the floor with her mouth open, oblivious to the cheerful chatter of the friendly housekeeper as she crossed to one of a pair of doors opposite a virtual bank of multipaned windows overlooking the street. A bench had been built in beneath the window and topped with a long, thick crimson velvet cushion, which matched the heavy draperies. Mrs. Baldwin spoke to her from the dressing room.

"You have some lovely things."

"Thank you."

She appeared in the doorway holding the sapphire blue dress that Avis had meant to wear the night before. "Now this is lovely," she said. "You see that you make him take you someplace worthy of it."

Avis laughed, caught off-guard by a surge of sheer joy. "I think he already has!"

Mrs. Baldwin beamed. "Oh, pish. This is nothing. He's rich as Midas, you know."

"I'm beginning to get that idea."

"And you didn't have it before?"

"Well, I knew he wasn't rubbing his last two nickels together, but this..." She shrugged helplessly. "I'm not sure I'm ready for this, frankly."

"Well, we are ready for you," Mrs. Baldwin told her unabashedly. Folding her hands, she clucked her tongue. "He's too much business since his wife died."

"You've known him a long time, it seems."

"He was a mite of four when he first walked through that door downstairs," the housekeeper said mistily. "I've loved him like my own ever since. I thought it would be the same with Nicholas, but..."

She looked so alarmed that Avis felt it important to say, "I know about Lucien's son."

Mrs. Baldwin relaxed enough to sniff disapprovingly, "The child never leaves San Francisco." Then she added grudgingly, "I suppose it's for the best." With that she disappeared back into the dressing room. "I'll have you unpacked in a twinkling, dear. Then maybe you'd like to see the kitchen? I'll warrant you're hungry again. I told him, scones and fruit are a poor substitute for eggs and ham, but does he listen to me? Has he ever? Ha."

Avis just smiled and looked around her again. A different world indeed and a frightening one in a way. Suddenly chilled, she chafed her arms through her sleeves, but then she shook her head. What was there to fear? She didn't for a moment believe that Lucien Tyrone or anyone in this household would harm her, and yet she couldn't help wondering if she hadn't made a mistake. She thought, briefly, about going straight back to the hotel, but she'd never be able to make herself do anything as rude as skipping out on her host without a word of explanation, and any explanation she might have made disappeared the moment Lucien Tyrone walked into the room some hours later and swept her into his arms.

"I won't be able to fit into my clothing if she keeps feeding me every hour on the hour," Avis complained good-naturedly. The past week had been a miracle of delights, not the least of which was Mrs. Baldwin's determined efforts to spoil her shamefully.

"But she's so very happy, having you to feed," Lucien teased, lifting the sponge and squeezing it so that warm water ran in rivulets down the slopes of her breasts. "Besides, Baldwin says you walked five miles today."

As she was sitting between his legs, Avis laid her head back on his shoulder. "There was so much to see! I never dreamed Westminster Abbey would be so fascinating. Emma says—"

"She's working out, then?" he interrupted pointedly. "You like her?"

"She's wonderful."

"I'm glad. You were unsure at first."

That was putting it mildly. She hadn't wanted him to hire a tour guide for her. They had almost argued about it, and she'd given in only reluctantly. Avis turned to face him now, sloshing sudsy water inside the enormous tub. "I was downright ungracious at first, and you know it."

He smiled and tapped the end of her nose with a wet forefinger. "A little matter of pride, I think. I rather like that about you." He showed her what else he liked, cupping her breasts with his hands.

She turned and placed her back to his chest once more, doing her best to ignore the heat building inside her as his hands filled themselves again. It was disconcerting, that heat, as it seemed to burn hotter with every passing day. She had convinced herself that desire would pall and quickly diminish as the days passed; instead, it had grown.

"Well, at the risk of inflating your already enormous ego," she said blithely, sinking down to lay her head on his shoulder so she could look up at him, "Emma is probably the best tour guide in all of England."

"Better than me?" he asked softly, bringing his mouth close to hers.

Avis chose to ignore that and tried not to gulp, saying lightly, "It's hard to believe that anyone so young could know so much."

"I try not to let it go to my head."

She elbowed him. "I was talking about Emma."

He chuckled, well aware of her meaning. "I'm glad she pleases you."

"I don't think pleasing me is really the issue," Avis said pointedly.

"Oh, but it is," he assured her, sliding his hands downward over her belly.

She gave him an arch look. "What I mean is that Emma is more interested in pleasing you than me. She has a serious crush on you, in case you haven't noticed. You're her second favorite subject, right after the monarchy."

He made a face and slid one hand lower still. "Scottish schoolgirls are not to my taste. I like my women from the Wild West these days."

These days. These days couldn't last much longer. She had been here a week already. Too many more and she would never want to go home again.

"We have theater tickets," she reminded him gently, grasping his clever fingers.

Undeterred, he nuzzled her ear. "They won't close the door to us, you know."

No one closed the door to Lucien Tyrone, not even her. Not yet. "I-I don't want to miss anything. Besides, I have a new dress to wear." She had worn the sapphire dress to dinner, as well as to a concert at the Royal Albert Hall, so she had devoted her afternoon to shopping for something new.

"Come then," he said, turning her in his arms and moving forward so that he could pull her legs about him. "Let's not waste any time."

She did as he wanted, did exactly as he wanted. It was so easy, so natural, to want to please him. As always she was astonished afterward at how easily and completely she had succumbed. "I don't know how you do this," she told him, floating bonelessly in a virtual sea of rapture, the minutes ticking away. They would be lucky to make the second act.

"I don't think that *I* do it," he said, from the corner of the tub where he had collapsed. "I think *we* do it. I think it's us, you and me together."

Us. A shiver lifted gooseflesh on her wet skin. She folded herself into a sitting position, pulled her feet beneath her and rose, languidly sluicing the water from her upper body before throwing a leg over the side of the tub and reaching for a towel. "*We* had better get a move on."

"Stop it," he said, moving to the outside edge.

She looked back at him in surprise, wrapping the towel around herself. "What?"

"Stop avoiding the subject."

"I'm not avoiding anything. I just don't want to miss the whole first act."

He frowned at her, watching with hooded eyes as she began to briskly towel-dry her hair. "I'm not going to let you get away with that forever, you know."

She blinked at him. "I don't have the foggiest idea what you're talking about."

"Don't you?"

She faced him, arms folded. "Are you spoiling for a fight, Lucien? Because I don't like to fight."

Something welled into his dark eyes. She thought for a moment that it might have been anger or even worry, but then a smile tugged at his lips. He rose from the water and reached for another of the towels that had been left warming in front of the fire. "I know you don't. It's one of the dearest and most frustrating things about you."

She tilted her head at him. "I don't understand."

"I think you do," he said, unabashedly naked. He toweled off, while she tried not to be affected by what she saw. As golden as she imagined Greece itself to be, he was a man of pure masculine prowess. "You hide behind that sweet exterior of yours," he went on. "I say, 'Don't go back to Texas. Stay with me,' and you smile and say, 'I want to.' But what you're really saying is, 'I won't.'"

She smiled apologetically. "That's not true. I do want to stay."

"Then do it," he said and dropped the towel.

Flustered, she finally looked away, saying softly, "No vacation lasts forever."

"No one suggested that it should."

"There you are then." She turned and moved toward the dressing room, which was a marvel filled not just by drawers and closets and benches and slipper chairs but a lighted cosmetics console and a sink as well. "I won't be long," she promised over her shoulder, only to find herself brought up short at the end of her own arm, his hand clamped firmly around her wrist.

"For the record," he said intently, "I do believe that you want to stay, and yet you won't. Why is that?"

For an instant, just for an instant, she considered telling him that she feared she needed him too much, but she had let herself be trapped that way once already, and she would not let it happen again, however tempting the trap might be. She pulled free of him, realized that she was teetering on the edge of panic and dropped her voice to a pleasant whisper. "Please don't ruin it, Lucien. We've had such a lovely time. You've been so generous and very, very sweet. That's how I want to remember you."

He literally bared his teeth as he reached out with one arm and swept her against him. "And you," he said, "are infuriating. Infuriating. Frustrating. Intoxicating."

He took her mouth, swooped down upon it. She didn't resist, couldn't hold back at all. He swept his tongue inside, time and again, fitting and refitting, bodies as well as lips. When he finally lifted his head, she looked up at him and softly said what she'd been putting off saying, "I'm leaving on Monday."

Three more days. No one said it, but the thought echoed around the room like a ricocheting bullet. His nostrils flared, and suddenly he curled his fingers around the top edge of her towel and tugged it away. "Then you can forget the damned theater."

It was already forgotten.

She capitulated eagerly once more, but it wasn't really about that. In an odd way, it was more about showing them both how much she could take, how much she could walk away from, for in the end walking away was her only choice. She knew it instinctively, had come to know it more and more every time they touched, that she could lose herself more completely to this man than she ever had to Kenneth. And that she must not.

Once already she'd given her life to a man, the life she should have had. That future, all those possibilities, had evaporated like so much smoke the moment she'd committed herself to Kenneth. She would never let that happen again. Edwin Searle had given her a second chance, and she couldn't squander that, but she feared that if she stayed too long with Luc, she would.

"I can't believe this." Luc gestured to the luggage littering his foyer and made a concerted effort to tamp down his temper. Aware of the Baldwins wringing their hands in the background, he pitched his voice low and stepped close to Avis. "We talked about this last night."

"Yes, we did," she conceded gently, "and I told you I couldn't stay."

''That was before—'' He bit back the words, glancing in the direction of the Baldwins.

They didn't need to know what had happened in the privacy of his bedroom the previous night, when he had dedicated long hours to pulling one gasped confession after another out of her. He was the best of lovers. He made her feel like the most beautiful and desirable woman in the world. London had become a magical experience for her. She felt pampered, appreciated, like a princess in a fairy tale, and she would love to stay in this beautiful house in this fascinating city for the next few weeks while he finished his business here. He had thought it was settled.

Basically, he had spent the whole of Sunday convincing her not to leave, and never had he been more charming, more solicitous, more appreciative. He'd arranged a private tour of Buckingham Palace, for pity's sake! He had taken her to lunch at the finest club in the city and watched her eyes widen as government ministers, rock stars and aristocrats had fawned over him. A viewing of one of the finest private art collections in the world had taken the afternoon, but the entire evening had been devoted to making love.

Every ounce of skill, every erotic technique, every romantic impulse he possessed had been employed with single-minded dedication until his repertoire, his mind and his body had been utterly exhausted. Deeply satisfied, he had gone to sleep believing that they would have weeks yet. Just that morning he had happily announced to Mrs. Baldwin that Avis would be staying, only to be called away from an important meeting less than two hours later by the panicked housekeeper with the news that Avis was on her way out the door! Confounded, he felt a fresh surge of anger, which he again fought to suppress.

"Avis," he began much more reasonably than seemed possible, "there is no good rationalization for you to return to Texas today."

She sighed and smiled that sweet, compliant smile that he was beginning to hate. "Lucien, it's time for me to go. I have a business and a life that I need to get back to, and I've already made the flight arrangements."

"I told you last night that I would put my private jet at your disposal when it was time."

"It is time, and I've already paid for the ticket."

"Forget the damned ticket!"

She spread her hands. "I can't do that."

"Can't?" he exploded. "You mean you won't!"

She bowed her head. "All right, I won't."

"Why?" he demanded. "Last night you said you wanted to stay!"

"I do."

He knew better than to think that he had won at this point. Thoroughly exasperated, he took her by the arm and steered her into the nearest room, which, by chance, was the formal sitting room. When they were alone, he pulled her into his arms. She went willingly, as she always did. "Why go when you want to stay?"

She brushed a hand across his chest and looked up at him. "Lucien, I can't expect my business partner to carry on indefinitely without me, and I can't live in a fantasy.''

He pulled her closer. ''This does not feel real to you?''

She smiled almost sadly. ''This has been a lovely dream, Lucien, a fabulous, almost unbelievable dream, but now it's time to wake up and get back to business.''

Business. If he understood anything, it was business, and this had nothing whatsoever to do with her business. His, however, was going to keep him right here in London for some time. Perhaps it was selfish of him to want her here with him, but he didn't really care, and he couldn't help feeling angry and, yes, hurt that she could so easily walk away.

''What can I say to make you stay?'' he asked softly, but she merely shook her head.

''I'm no happier about it than you are, but it's time for me to go. It's really just that simple.''

He almost laughed. This was anything but simple, and if she thought she could walk away from him this easily, she was very sadly mistaken. Short of locking her in a closet, however, he had no other option at present than to let her go. For now. He released her and walked over to lean against a table that had once graced the home of King George II.

''You are still a puzzle to me,'' he admitted tautly, ''a beautiful, compelling puzzle.''

She lifted her hands as if confused. ''What is it you think I'm keeping from you?''

''Why you insist on going when you really want to stay.''

"But I've told you over and over." She bowed her head, wrapping her arms tightly around her slender middle. "Please, Lucien, let's not do this. I don't want to miss my flight, and I don't want to part on bad terms, not after the incredible holiday you've given me."

He breathed deeply through his nostrils and finally nodded. Defeat always left a very bitter taste in his mouth, but it never lingered for long because the success to follow was always so very sweet. Meanwhile, it was time for a strategic retreat. He opened his arms. "Come and give me a proper good-bye then."

As always, she almost flew to him. He made it a kiss that she would never forget. When he released her, tears stood in her eyes, but determination was there, as well. He found, to his surprise, that he could not easily speak again, so he stayed where he was while she hurried from the room. When she suggested to Baldwin that it might be best if she called a cab, his trusted driver sounded understandably and predictably horrified, so Lucien put him out of his misery by walking to the door and giving him a nod. Then he turned back into the room and stayed there until she had departed his house. He was not surprised to find Mrs. Baldwin standing behind him when he turned again, a militant look in her disapproving eye.

"I can't believe you just let her go."

"I did not just let her go, Hettie," he retorted more sharply than he intended. "I never let go of anything that is mine. You know that." She suddenly beamed at him, a reaction he found inexplicable until he re-thought those words. "Now, don't go planning any wedding,'' he ordered impatiently. ''I'm simply not ready to let go of her yet.''

''Does she know that?''

''She'll know soon enough.''

''My, my,'' the housekeeper said smugly, ''she's really worked up a head of steam in you, hasn't she? You'll pardon my saying so, but your mother's not going to like that.''

''I will not pardon your saying so, and it's no more my mother's business whom I choose to sleep with than it is yours.''

Hettie just smiled, damn her. ''There now,'' she said soothingly, ''I'll make you a nice shepherd's pie for dinner. That'll make you feel better.''

He smiled despite himself, but it was going to take a lot more than a good dinner to make this night better. He wouldn't even think of the weeks ahead.

Chapter Six

Avis stared at the bound, printed prospectus. The soft, blue cover folded back in a roll perfectly suited to her left hand. The neat black letters and colored charts practically jumped off the crisp, stark white page, but try as she might, and despite a degree of natural expertise, she hadn't been able to decipher a word thus far. The thing might as well have been written in Greek.

Greek.

Sudden remembrance washed over her in waves: Lucien dropping smoothly down into the airplane seat next to her. Lucien smiling gaily, his dark eyes heated with sensual intent. Lucien above her, driving into her, his flexible mouth moving over hers, long-fingered, square-nailed hands molding her flesh. Wet, golden skin. Hard muscles. Lucien cradling her in his arms, his heart beating beneath her cheek. Lucien. Lucien. Lucien.

She dropped the prospectus and covered her face with her hands. For nearly a month she had been unexpectedly carried off by these unwanted memories. It wasn't supposed to be like this. London should have faded into a safe, pleasurable recollection that could be taken out, dusted off and enjoyed at her leisure, not this *ambush* of relived sensation. What was wrong with her? Why couldn't she manage this? Just how self-destructive was she?

The telephone on her dark, shiny desktop rang. She jerked, then snatched up the wireless receiver with a helpless sense of relief. Bringing it to her right ear, she rotated her chair, turning her back to the door. "Avis Lorimer."

"Hey!"

Sierra's happy voice pierced Avis to the heart. "Hey, yourself. How's married life?"

"Amazing. Oh, my gosh, Avis, I am so lucky. Sam is just…*amazing*."

Amazing is about six-two, blond and half Greek. Avis turned off that treacherous thought by asking, "How are you feeling?"

"Never better. And how about you?"

"Oh, I'm fine, just busy."

"We've noticed that," Sierra said lightly. "Haven't seen much of you in the past few weeks. We've barely even heard about your trip. Please say you'll come to dinner."

"Of course, I'll come to dinner. I'd love to come to dinner. Just as soon as I can."

"How's Friday?"

The polite thing would have been to say yes, but somehow she couldn't make herself do it. Instead, she stalled by turning in her chair and checking her desk calendar. "Friday. Friday." The page was blank, but she didn't let that influence her answer. "Mmm, I really should attend this business thing on Friday evening. Sorry. You know how it is." She made a mental note to call Pete as soon as she hung up with Sierra and rescind her refusal to accompany him to a certain cocktail party.

"Okay," Sierra said. "Saturday then."

Avis pinched the bridge of her nose and resorted to an outright lie. "I'm taking Gwyn to dinner on Saturday." She grimaced at the silence that followed and added lamely, "You know she doesn't get out enough."

"Avis," Sierra asked softly, "are you avoiding me?"

"Goodness, no. Don't be silly."

Her office door opened, and her partner Pete breezed through it, speaking. "Avis, can you...oh, sorry."

She couldn't have been happier to see him. "Sierra, my partner just came in. I have to go. Listen, I'll call you in a few days, and we'll set something up. Okay?" She hung up quickly and literally beamed at Pete, who seemed taken aback.

Something about him always put her in mind of the actor Spencer Tracy. He was an attractive man by anyone's standards, taller than average with the build and mannerisms of a heavyweight boxer, piercing blue eyes and a thick head of prematurely silver hair that showed only traces of its original medium brown. Most importantly, he was a smart, savvy business-man. If she had a complaint it was that he tended to let his social life spill over into business, something with which he himself had no problem. Indeed, he often tried to entice her to do the same. And now she was about to accommodate him.

"What can I do for you, Pete?"

He scratched his ear uncertainly. "Uh, could you dig out your Hollow Ridge file so I can copy it? Guess I left mine at home."

"Sure." She rose and walked to the bank of file cabinets along one wall. Within moments, she had extracted the requested file and was holding it out to him.

"Thanks," he said, taking it from her hand. "Don't know where my brain was this morning." He opened the folder and began thumbing through it.

"I know what you mean," she told him. "I'm hav-ing trouble concentrating myself today."

He looked up at her words. "Everything okay?"

She wrinkled her nose, hating herself. "I think I've just been working too much lately."

He closed the folder and lowered it. "You have been hitting it pretty hard since you got back from London," he agreed. "It's like you have to work twice as hard to make up for going off and having a little fun. I keep telling you that you need to loosen up."

She smoothed the lay of her collarless, buff-colored suit jacket and forced a smile. "I think you're right. In fact, if the offer's still open, I just might go with you to that party on Friday, after all.''

Clearly stunned, he gaped at her so long that she had to fight to keep from nervously plucking at the creases of her slacks.

''Great!'' Pete finally reacted. ''That's great! What, uh, made you change your mind?''

She looked away and moved back toward her desk. ''Guess I'm just feeling a little restless.''

That was true, but what she didn't, couldn't, tell him was that she was avoiding one of her best friends. Sierra and Sam had married while she was in London, and she couldn't be happier about it, especially since they were expecting a baby, but just watching the happy couple together made her ache with an emptiness that she hated yet couldn't hold at bay. All she seemed able to do about it was keep her distance until her emotions somehow got back on an even keel, and if that meant nursing a single drink for hours at a crowded, boring cocktail party with a weary smile pasted on her face, well, so be it.

While Pete chatted excitedly about who would be there and what a good time they would have, Avis made herself listen and nod at all the appropriate moments, until finally he swept out of her office behind a gleaming white grin. She felt like a grade-A heel, but that didn't stop her from picking up the telephone and calling Gwyn Dunstan to make a dinner date for Saturday night.

Of the friendly group of four women who had operated small businesses out of the strip mall that Edwin Searle had patronized, only Gwyn had not been named in the will, and she had adamantly refused to let the other three cut her in, despite the fact that she worked long and hard to make a minimal living from the coffee shop where the four had once gathered on a daily basis. Now both Val and Sierra were happily married, which seemed to leave Avis and Gwyn with a special bond. It was only natural that Avis should spend more time with her than the other two.

Gwyn gladly agreed to meet her but insisted that a simple pizza would suit her better than steak or a hamburger. Besides, her two teenagers would be thrilled when she brought the leftovers home to them. Avis laughed and said they'd have to order a large pie, then, maybe even one apiece. She didn't realize how very much she was looking forward to spending time with Gwyn until after she hung up the phone, but then why should that bother her? It wasn't as if she was lonely, after all, just unsettled.

The weeks had simultaneously flown and crept by, busy yet somehow empty, too. Soon the paralyzing heat of summer would be upon them, and she found herself dreading it this year as she never had before. Maybe she ought to think about going someplace cool. Like London. No. She quickly put that thought away and walked around her desk. Picking up the prospectus again, she reached for a pen. She was going to get the numbers she needed out of this thing if it killed her. And then she would find something else to do and something else after that until one day thoughts of London would bring only the same vague pleasure as any standard holiday memory.

* * *

"Girl, you look like a million bucks," Gwyn drawled, a hand perched on her slender hip, "which puts you in the same category as your bank account." She laughed and flopped her hand from the wrist before plopping her blue-jean-clad bottom onto the red vinyl seat of the booth. "Then again, you always looked like a queen slumming."

"Thanks," Avis said dubiously, wishing she'd worn denim instead of plum silk. "You're looking pretty good yourself. I like your hair down. I don't think I realized how long it is."

Gwyn grinned and preened like a schoolgirl, her cool gray eyes sparkling as she confided, "Molly insisted that I wear it down. She says I don't make the most of what I've got, like I care when I'm hauling it out at 3:00 a.m."

Gwyn's business required long hours and hard work, which accounted for her firm, lean look and the minimalist approach she seemed to take with her appearance. As usual, Gwyn hadn't worn a shred of makeup, but her thick, biscuit-brown hair hanging board-straight from a side part to the bottoms of her shoulder blades made her look much younger than her thirty-six years, an effect bolstered by her customary attire, which consisted of a simple T-shirt, running shoes and blue jeans.

"Well, Molly's right about the hair," Avis said, "but I understand what you're saying."

The lack of a scraped-back ponytail wasn't the only change that Avis detected about her friend, however. In many ways, the hard edge that seemed so much a part of her personality had lost some of its sharpness during this past year, and in a strange way, Avis supposed they had Edwin Searle to thank for that, too. Gwyn, like the rest of them, had started to change when she'd come to terms with Edwin's will.

"So, what've you been up to?" Gwyn asked.

Avis made a face. "Working, working and working, with the exception of one very boring cocktail party, which was also work-related. Bankers, by the way, are not exactly party animals. But enough about me. How're you doing? Kids okay? Business good?"

"Kids are fine," Gwyn answered. "Business is so-so, but we're hanging in. As for me, I'm good." She smiled and folded her firm, slender arms against the tabletop. "We had this conversation right after you got back from London, if you remember, so let's skip to the chase. Sierra says you're avoiding her."

Avis threw up her hands and plopped back in her seat. "I am not avoiding her! I'm busy. I…" She stopped, propped her elbows on the table and dropped her head into her hands. "All right, I'm avoiding her." She looked up again. "It's not that I don't care or don't want to spend time with Sierra or…or Val, for that matter. It's just that Sierra has Sam now and Val has Ian, and I-I just feel…"

"Left out," Gwyn supplied knowingly. "Alone."

"No," Avis said firmly. "I prefer alone. I *treasure* alone. I wouldn't change my life for anything. It's just…oh, I don't know what's the matter with me."

Gwyn clucked her tongue soothingly and reached across the table to pat Avis's forearm. "There, there, honey. I didn't mean it that way, like you're lonely or anything. Heck, you've got us, me especially, and

I know something's been bothering you. Why don't you tell me about it?''

Avis sighed. "I don't know where to begin. It's all so confusing."

"Why not try starting with London?"

Avis looked up sharply, but before she could form a reply, a waitress approached with water glasses and an order pad. They chose two salads and a large sausage pie with pineapple.

"I can hear Chip now," Gwyn said with a grin, referring to her thirteen-year-old son. "'Yuck! Pineapple! *Girlie* pizza.'"

"That won't keep him from eating it, though," Avis predicted.

"He'll be shoving it in while he's complaining."

They both laughed. Then Gwyn leveled her gaze. "Come on, kiddo, tell me about London, and I don't mean Buckingham Palace."

"What makes you think this has anything to do with London?" Avis hedged.

"Oh, I don't know. Maybe it's because you went over there the same Avis we've always known and came back different somehow."

Avis bit her lip and softly said, "I met a man."

Gwyn sighed. "I should've known."

"What do you mean?"

Gwyn smiled. "I mean that it's obviously your turn. First, Val found Ian. Then Sierra found Sam. Stands to reason you'd be next. My luck, I'll get left out of this deal, too."

"No!" Avis insisted. "That's not it, at all. I don't want a man. You know that."

"I know that's what you think."

"That's how it is," Avis insisted, but Gwyn lifted a hand.

"Why don't you just tell me about it?"

Avis nodded glumly. She had never intended to tell anyone what had really happened in London. It was meant to be her guilty little secret, a figurative pint of ice cream to be gobbled in privacy at moments of weakness or indulgence. Somehow, though, she found that she couldn't enjoy her hoard of memories. Maybe it would help if she shared it.

"This is just between us," she warned, and took a deep breath. "We met on the airplane going over. He's a widower, part Greek, and yes, he looks like one of those ancient statues carved in marble, too beautiful to believe. He's wealthy and charming, thirty-six, and I stayed with him all but the very first night I was there."

Gwyn's eyes had grown wide as the words had tumbled out of Avis's mouth. She blinked at that last bit of information and blew out a short breath. "Well. He must be something. I mean, I've seen you hit on by all types."

Avis rolled her eyes. "You have not."

"Oh, yes, I have. You just haven't bothered to notice. That's the point. Any man who could grab your attention has to have something major going on."

"That's one way of putting it," Avis muttered, and Gwyn laughed.

"Come on. I want a blow-by-blow account."

To Avis's surprise, the story spilled out in one continuous flow. She kept the intimate details to herself and still told more than she'd intended. The salads came, and then the pizza, but neither slowed her narrative, and when she was done, she somehow felt different. In a strange way, she felt warmer, as if she'd been chilled and stiff inside for all these weeks and talking about it had loosened up the blood flow to her emotions once again. It proved to be a two-edged sword, however, as suppressed feelings crowded her. She tired to shake them off, but they came so swiftly that she couldn't even identify them, let alone control them. Shaking her head, she finished up her long tale. "Anyway, I had to come home. So here I am. And that's it."

Gwyn stared at the half-eaten piece of pizza on her plate and shook her head. "I don't think so."

Avis frowned. "What do you mean? It was a vacation romance. Now it's over."

"Why?"

Avis stared at her friend with dismay. "I was on *vacation*. It was time to come home. I had to end it."

"Oh, come on. You know you weren't ready for that."

"I was ready," Avis insisted softly, desperately. "No one forced me to leave when I did. I chose the time. I made the reservations."

"Then what's the problem?"

Avis looked at Gwyn helplessly. "I don't know."

Gwyn studied her for a moment, choosing her words carefully. "He excited you, and that must have been frightening, given your history." Avis's frown deepened, but Gwyn leaned forward and went on, lowering her voice. "You've beat yourself up enough

over Kenneth. It's time you learned to trust yourself
again.'' Avis began shaking her head, but Gwyn was
determined to have her say. "You never had anything
to be ashamed of there, honey. You were a baby, for
pity's sake. He was much, much older, a professor,
more sophisticated. I know you felt responsible. I
know your brother held you responsible. But you
made the only choice you felt you could, and then
you lived with it. You did the right thing, as you saw
it, and you paid a stiff price. Trust what you've
learned as a result, and give yourself some credit, for
pity's sake.''

"That's what I'm doing,'' Avis hissed. "That's exactly why I had to come home.'' She sighed and admitted, "In some ways, Lucien was an even bigger
mistake than Kenneth, and as soon as I realized that,
I couldn't get away fast enough.''

Gwyn's expression verged on pity. "If that's so,
then why are you grieving?''

Grieving. The truth of it hit Avis like a ton of
bricks, and it was as if she plunged into a deep well
of sadness. Or perhaps she had been floundering
around in that well for the last month or so, only just
now realizing it. She wished she hadn't.

Gwyn smiled wanly. "I've seen that look in your
eye before, first when Kenneth died, then when Edwin did. But this…all I really know for sure is that
he got to you in a big way.''

Avis blinked back sudden tears. "You're right. Lucien did get to me, like no one else ever has, but don't
you see? That's all the more reason to end it and get
back to my life here.''

"But isn't that just running away, Avis?"

Avis stared at her friend for a long time. "Maybe," she finally conceded, "but you don't know how many times I've wished I'd had the strength to run from Kenneth. So much would have been different."

"Different maybe," Gwyn argued, "but you don't know that it would have been better."

"I know I wouldn't have disappointed my brother," Avis said softly. "I know Kenneth wouldn't have been forced out of his teaching career. I know Ellis wouldn't have hated me for taking away his father's attention."

"Avis," Gwyn said urgently, "you were twenty years old."

"Stop saying that. It's no excuse."

"You needed someone to love you."

"And I've learned never to let myself be that needy again," Avis stated firmly.

Gwyn slumped for a moment, but then she nodded, sat back and pointedly changed the subject. "Have you heard what our illustrious mayor's been saying about Sam and Sierra?"

Even as Avis cringed at the thought of fresh rumors, she smiled in gratitude for the change in topic. "What now?"

"The new story, and I know for a fact that Heston Witt is floating it, is that Sierra's baby might not even be Sam's, but he's claiming it in order to get Sierra's money."

Avis shook her head in disgust. "And people are buying that tripe?"

Gwyn shrugged. "Probably not, but that doesn't keep them from passing it around."

"What did people in Puma Springs gossip about before Edwin made that will?"

Gwyn chuckled. "Yeah, he gave you, Sierra and Val a million-plus each, but he gave the town years worth of grist for the gossip mills." She waved a hand dismissively. "They're just jealous. I should know." Her self-deprecating smile pinched Avis.

"Gwyn, you're such a good friend. It's not fair—"

"Oh, now, don't start that again," Gwyn interrupted. "Like I said in the beginning, it is what it's supposed to be, and to tell you the truth, I'm not sure I'd trade places with any of you. I see what the inheritance has brought with it, the gossip, the scrutiny, the envy, the kooks and mooches. Yeah, I get tired of stretching a buck, but I don't have the patience to put up with all the junk you and Sierra and Val have." She shook her head. "No, I don't envy y'all the inheritance, not considering everything that comes with it, anyway. Now, on the other hand, Ian and Sam are pretty cute." She grinned and wiggled an eyebrow. "I would happily get in the way of something like that."

Avis laughed. "You lie. You're no more interested in men than I am."

"That," said Gwyn softly, "is unfortunately true. The problem is, you're more interested than you want to admit, at least in one man."

Avis clamped her mouth shut at that, and Gwyn, bless her, decided it was time to signal the waitress for a take-out box for the leftover pizza and, since they'd really eaten very little of the meal, she insisted that they should have dessert, too. Avis happily agreed, and they shared a piece of turtle cheesecake dripping with caramel, chocolate and pecans before going their separate ways. Alone.

Chapter Seven

Avis stared through the window overlooking downtown Fort Worth and the popular Sundance Square, with its shops, restaurants, clubs and art galleries. The traffic on the street seemed as desultory and lethargic as she felt, but she supposed that was normal for a weekday afternoon. Then again, time itself seemed to be dragging listlessly of late. The past week and more had crept by with nerve-wracking tedium.

Time and again she had reached for the telephone, only to draw back for reasons she couldn't quite explain even to herself. During the course of her marriage, she'd been somewhat isolated, having little in common with Kenneth's few friends and limited opportunities for making her own. During his illness, Kenneth had contented himself with his books and his collections, she had stayed occupied with the hobby shop and seeing to his care. After his death she had felt terribly alone. Money had been tight, and life had felt like a continuous struggle, but she'd made friends of the other businesswomen at the strip mall and gradually had come to feel liberated. That was no longer the case. Now, while her friends were concerned with their families and other responsibilities, she had only her work. In many ways she seemed more isolated than ever simply because the Searle inheritance made it impossible for her to trust new acquaintances easily.

She hated feeling lonely. She hated even the word, but she could find no other more appropriate for the dissatisfaction that consumed her. She turned abruptly from the window, realizing with a start that she was not actually alone.

Of course she was not alone. Pete had come into the office some minutes earlier and had been reading aloud to her from a long e-mail message that he had just received. And she hadn't heard a word. Not that he seemed to notice, if his sudden whoop was any indication. He threw his arms into the air, tossing the papers exuberantly. The three closely typed pages wafted to the floor.

"Do you know what this means?" he exclaimed jubilantly. She didn't have a clue, so she just smiled benignly. "We're going to get the TexBank redevelopment!"

The TexBank redevelopment project involved the acquisition and refurbishment of a forty-story downtown office tower substantially damaged by a direct-hit tornado some three years earlier. The building had been abandoned by its owner, one of the largest banking institutions in the state, and the insurer who'd retained possession of it, had been trying to rid itself of the damaged property ever since. Debate had raged over whether or not to tear down the building due to the extensive damage to its glass skin and interior or refurbish the existing steel superstructure, which city inspectors had judged sound. Ardent proponents of refurbishment pointed out that the cost of deconstructing and rebuilding would be substantially higher than that of restoration, say seventy-five million as opposed to sixty, but in a tough economy sixty mil had proven as difficult to come by as seventy-five.

That hadn't stopped Pete from dreaming. He'd found a bright young architect in Austin, who had some startlingly innovative plans which he insisted could be executed for a mere fifty-six million dollars. After two years of promotion, Pete was still thirty million short of the goal. Avis had assumed that he'd given up on the idea. The gleam in his eyes now said otherwise.

"This could put us in the big league, Avis!"

The biggest deal they'd ever done had required a measly fifteen million dollars in investment, and she knew that he expected her to show some enthusiasm for the TexBank project, but somehow she couldn't seem to muster up any. For one thing, she didn't understand what was going on yet. Walking across the carpeted floor toward her desk, she bent and swept up the papers one-by-one, asking, "Do you mind if I keep these and take another look?"

He laughed. ''Look all you want, partner! Meanwhile, I'm going to check out Corydon.''

Corydon. That must be the company who had expressed interest in the deal. Avis nodded, quickly perusing the printed e-mail while Pete ran from the office in his eagerness to prove that Corydon was on the level. Leaning a hip against the corner of her desk, Avis carefully dissected the missive word for tiny word.

Corydon described itself as a fairly small but aggressive New York investment firm specializing in reclamations. It was aware of the TexBank situation, having learned of the project through a shared line-of-credit lender, and boasted almost limitless investment funds. Since Corydon deemed TexBank a prime investment opportunity, they were interested in pursuing a limited partnership. It requested a convenient date for a company rep to call in person to discuss the possibility of a joint venture. The name at the bottom of the letter was Charles Anthony Daniels, CEO.

Avis arched both brows at the familiar name. Daniels was a well-known financier, as famous for his flamboyance as his cagey investments. If Daniels was really involved, the thing would be easy enough to check out and undoubtedly legitimate. Well, well. Pete just might get his big deal, after all. She smiled, happy for him, and wondered why the feeling seemed so flat. But if her feet remained firmly stuck in the doldrums, his did not.

Pete could barely get his head out of the clouds, especially after Corydon checked out as expected. As

the day for a face-to-face meeting with a Corydon
representative drew nearer, Pete only grew more ex-
uberant, bouncing around the office on the balls of
his feet, laughing and talking up the project. By Friday, he could barely contain himself.

"Monday," he exclaimed, perched on the corner
of her desk with a grin. "Sweet, merciful heaven!
Can you believe it? Suppose Charles Anthony Daniels himself will come?"

"I wouldn't know. Haven't they said?"

"Not really."

"Well, I wouldn't worry about it."

"Wouldn't you like to meet Daniels, though?"

"I never expected to. This is your deal, Pete. Coeli
Development was working on this long before C&L
came into being."

"Coeli Development *is* C&L Investments and Development," Pete insisted.

"But it's a limited partnership. You're free to operate independently."

"Why should I? This is a huge project, Avis. I
need you on this. Don't bail on me now."

"I don't have the passion for this that you do,"
she admitted softly.

"So?" He hunched a shoulder and popped down
onto the corner of her desk. "You have the brains
and style for it. The suggestions you made to Rifkin
were spectacular. Even he thought so, and he's shot
down every change in the plan that I've suggested
since we first hooked up." He pecked a finger on the
top of her desk. "This is a C&L I&D job, and that's
all there is to it. No more talk of opting out. Okay?"

He shrugged, not quite his ebullient self. "Whatever you say."

She folded her arms. "Now don't start worrying just because the meeting's going to be a day later than planned."

"It's just that I wore my good suit today," he groused with a grin. "Now I've either got to go home and change, wear something less impressive or charm my dry cleaners into giving me a fresh press tonight."

She had to admit that he looked very attractive in the stylish black suit and pale gray shirt and tie, the color of which brought out the distinguished silver of his thick, straight hair and the vibrant blue of his eyes. Though a little too heavily featured to be classically handsome, he did possess a rather dominant aura of masculinity. Not for the first time she wondered why it was that she couldn't feel something more than friendship for Pete. A mutual acquaintance had once described him as a cross between a teddy bear and a shark, and that wasn't far off the mark. She liked, trusted and respected Pete. Might it not become more if she gave it a chance?

"Run on home and change," she advised. "In fact, why don't you take the day off? You're not going to be any good around here now anyway."

He brightened. "I just might do that. It's a great day for a game of golf."

"There you go."

"Why don't you join me?"

She wrinkled her nose. "Golf's not my thing." She wondered briefly if she should go shopping for something to wear to dinner, but then she owned a couple of dresses that she'd never worn anywhere. Except London. She pushed aside the pang that such thoughts still elicited even after all these weeks and firmly made up her mind to wear something from her closet.

Pete turned toward the door, but it opened before he got to it, and their perpetually late secretary/receptionist Candy breezed into the small antechamber that was their lobby, her short, platinum-streaked hair standing on end in a fashionable spike.

"Is Mr. What's-his-name here yet?"

"Meeting's canceled," Pete announced glumly.

"Until tomorrow evening," Avis amended, seeing Candy's horrified expression.

"Tomorrow evening at the Lariat Club," Pete added with a wag of his brows.

Candy brightened immediately. "Ooh. The Lariat Club. Did you suggest that?"

Pete scratched an ear. "Uh, no, actually, they did. I had an e-mail this morning."

"Well, somebody's got good taste."

"Wouldn't expect anything else," Pete insisted. "Well, I'm out of here. See you tomorrow." He exited the suite with a jaunty wave.

"Where's he going?" Candy asked, dumping her enormous handbag behind the sleek, ebony counter that hid her messy desk.

"Taking the day off," Avis muttered, thinking of something else. "By the way, what is his name, this guy from Corydon?" Seemed to her that they ought to know by now.

Candy shrugged. ''Dunno. All their e-mails since the first one are signed the same way, just Corydon, Inc.''

''Haven't you spoken to anyone at Corydon?''

''Once, but all he said when he called was, 'This is Corydon, Inc.''''

''Well, who do you ask for when you call there?''

''Never called there. Never had to.''

''I see, and Pete hasn't mentioned a name?''

''Not to me.''

Avis tried not to frown. What difference did it make anyway? She put the small detail of the Corydon rep's name out of mind, except to wonder if it might actually be Daniels himself. It didn't seem likely, but given that she couldn't rule out the possibility, she decided she'd best dress for the dinner meeting with great care. She spent the rest of the day trying not to think about where she had worn each appropriate garment in her closet. And with whom.

That evening she made herself take an inventory of her wardrobe. The gown she had bought in London and never worn was too formal. The violet had bagged a little and should be cleaned. She laid it out to drop off at the dry cleaners. She passed over another as too heavy for spring and rejected unilaterally the little black dress that she had worn to the cocktail party. She considered one or two others purchased for the summer but ultimately came back to her favorite sapphire blue, as she had known she would.

It was two dresses really, attached just at the sides. The underdress was strapless and made of that wondrous knit that clung to the body like second skin.

Anything more than seamless pantyhose worn beneath it would show, even through the sheer, fitted overdress, the decided Oriental flare of which was demonstrated in the Mandarin collar and long, tight sleeves trimmed at the wrists with delicate, dyed-to-match embroidery. The bodice buttoned at a slant with tiny, odd-shaped bits of sapphire glass like rough-cut, polished stone, from left shoulder to below the right breast, and both under- and overskirts were slit on the left side almost from the hip to the knee-length hem. With nude stockings and embroidered, pointed-toed, high-heeled mules, she never felt better or more lavishly dressed than when wearing this unique ensemble.

She had worn this dress twice for Lucien, and both times he had undressed her afterward, working the tiny glass chips through the delicate holes one breathless button at time, then sliding the bodice from her shoulders and shoving the underdress to her waist. Before he'd finished, he had turned both the dress and her inside out.

Yes, it had to be this dress, if only to invest it with less poignant memories.

She wondered, to her surprise, what Pete might think of her in this. Shaking her head, she laid it aside and took herself downstairs to dine on canned soup and crackers.

The bulk of the evening was devoted to an orgy of grooming, beginning with a facial. She scrubbed, plucked, exfoliated, clarified and creamed, before dealing with her hair. It always behaved better the day after washing, and she wanted to look her best for Pete's sake, so she shampooed and conditioned and brushed until it dried glossy and full. That done, she softened her hands and feet with paraffin baths, then waxed her legs and, finally, applied frosty pink polish to her finger and toe nails.

By the time she slipped into bed she felt delightfully clean and feminine. Sleep, thankfully, was not then long in coming.

She woke the next morning to sunshine and optimism. The thought came to her out of nowhere that this was going to be a life-changing day. C&L was on the verge of big things. Some of Pete's enthusiasm for the TexBank project began to permeate the odd gloom in which she'd been floundering. They were going to negotiate a deal tonight that would eventually make them both very wealthy, not that the money really mattered. It was success, achievement, that she wanted now. For so long she had merely existed, now she was finally her own person, with a chance to prove what she could do, and she had the late Edwin Searle and good old Pete to thank for it. She wasn't going to disappoint either of them. Throwing back the covers, she hopped out of bed.

Looking forward to an excellent dinner, she skimped on breakfast and lunch while diligently studying the TexBank prospectus. Intending to do her partner proud, she determined to learn every detail of the project. Corydon, Inc. would leave the table tonight knowing that C&L I&D was very much on the ball.

In late afternoon she put aside the paperwork and went upstairs to get dressed. At precisely seven

o'clock, she walked down the stairs, a small silk
handbag tucked under one arm, hair coiled and
twirled artfully. Fifty-five minutes later, she walked
into the opulent marble and chrome foyer of the renowned Lariat Club and told the maître d' that she
was meeting two gentlemen.

He tugged at the cuffs of his plain white shirt beneath his black coat sleeves, and Avis noticed that he
wore a black string tie and alligator cowboy boots
with the tuxedo that comprised his uniform. ''Ms.
Lorimer?'' he inquired politely.

She was not surprised that she was expected.
''Yes.''

''This way please.''

He immediately turned and led her through a bev-
eled-glass door. As she followed, she glanced around
unobtrusively, taking in the eclectic mix of horn
chandeliers, tanned hides, chrome sculptures and
chili-pepper-red table linens and rugs. They wound
past a massive stone fireplace and a burbling fountain
then a pierced tin screen overlaid with copper figures
before the maître d' stopped in front of her and
bowed slightly.

''Gentlemen.''

Avis heard the sound of chair legs scraping across
granite. Then her escort stepped to one side and lifted
an arm toward the sheltered table. All charming gentility and feminine confidence, Avis smiled at him
and turned her head.

Her heart stopped.

Every molecule of oxygen escaped her lungs.

She shook her head disbelievingly.

For a long moment, no one said a word, but then Pete anxiously stepped forward and cupped her elbow with his big hand as if she were a fragile old lady who needed his help to cross the street. She felt herself begin to tremble.

"Avis," he said, an urgent edge to his voice, "I'd like you to meet Lucien Tyrone."

Chapter Eight

"Hello, Avis."

Twin waves of longing and panic hit her from different directions. She spluttered for a moment, overwhelmed. "L-Lucien?"

Luc ignored her discomfiture and raked her from head to toe with an assessing gaze. "You're looking splendid, as usual."

She finally got her bearings. "What are you doing here?"

A smile flitted across his mouth. "Conducting business, of course."

Corydon. It slapped her like a cold hand, boggling her mind and at the same time implanting definite information. He had known with whom he was dealing. He had planned it this way. She trembled now with outrage as much as horrifying delight. Stepping away from Pete, she laid her handbag onto the table. "Funny, you never said anything about a company called Corydon."

Lucien calmly smoothed his silk tie. "It's a recent acquisition, very recent, as it happens."

Pete emitted a nervous chuckle. "Turns out old Luc here actually bought the company from Daniels immediately after he approached us."

"Oh, I'm sure the deal was struck beforehand," Avis said, quietly seething now. What did this mean for Pete's dream of TexBank?

"As a matter of fact, it was," Lucien admitted easily. "May we sit now?" He reached over and pulled out a chair for her.

Avis hesitated a moment, torn between walking, running away and Pete's hopes. Finally, she dropped down into the chair, telling herself that she had to find out whether or not the TexBank deal was viable or if this was merely some terrible ruse on Lucien's part. Punishment for her leaving him perhaps? The men took their seats.

A waiter appeared and placed a filled water goblet in front of Avis, followed by an empty wineglass, into which he poured a fruity red wine.

"I've taken the liberty of ordering for all three of us," Lucien said smoothly. "I feel certain you won't be disappointed."

"Are you kidding?" Pete said heartily. "The chef here is renowned."

"So I am told." Lucien picked up his own wineglass and drank. He smoothed his napkin across his lap. Avis didn't look at him, but she felt his gaze on her. "How have you been?"

Her mind was whirling so quickly that she couldn't manage to open her mouth at first, but then Pete cleared his throat and touched her ankle with the toe of his shoe beneath the table. She caught her breath, swallowed and softly answered. "Fine. And you?"

"Busy."

"And your son? How is Nicholas?"

He shifted in his seat. "As well as can be expected."

"He must miss you when you're gone."

Lucien's smile was fleeting and tinged with concern, but his reply seemed flippant. "Perhaps. It did not seem so when I left him this morning. He was preoccupied with his finger painting."

She folded her arms across her waist and said nothing more. After an awkward pause, Pete bluffly asked, "So, how do you two know each other?"

Lucien sipped from his glass again before saying carefully, "We met quite by chance."

"Oh? Where?"

Lucien smiled at Pete's unsubtle prodding. That smile held something lupine. Avis briefly closed her eyes, certain that Lucien was about to announce their affair. Instead he said, "I had the great good fortune of touring London at the same time as Ms. Lorimer."

"Ah." Pete weighted that single syllable with a wealth of understanding.

"Imagine my delight," Lucien went on, "when I discovered that she was part of your company."

She shot him a look from beneath her lashes. "Yes, what a coincidence."

Pete could be heard gulping from his glass. "Small world, isn't it?"

"Very small," Lucien stated flatly. The appetizer arrived just then, shrimp in pastry cups filled with a spicy salsa jelly. Lucien smiled expansively, the gracious host. "Let's eat first and discuss business later, shall we?"

Pete hummed awkwardly over the tasty concoction, but Avis merely nibbled at hers, forcing out appropriate sounds. They followed that pattern through a salad of chopped jicama, peppers, pecans and corn on a bed of lettuce with an avocado dressing, a soup course of spicy creamed pumpkin laced with cinnamon and a main dish of pork and rice roasted inside a ring of oranges and jalapenos in a stingingly hot and superbly sweet sauce, in addition to side dishes of *charro* beans, squash and hearts of palm. It was a superb meal which Avis could do little more than taste while Lucien sent her silent glances and Pete chattered with nervous determination, mostly about TexBank and what an excellent project it was. By the time the waiter placed dessert before them—a praline flan with a plantain crust accompanied by coffee— Avis felt strung as tightly as a barbed-wire fence and Pete had come to the end of his patience.

"So," he asked, twirling his fork, "what do you think about the project?"

While Avis held her breath, Lucien dabbed at the corners of his mouth and replaced his napkin in his lap. "The plan is definitely innovative, but four floors of mall space is a lot of shopping when the retail rental market is depressed nationwide.''

Pete shifted in his seat. "That's true. However, Fort Worth is underserved in that area, and I have the figures to prove it.''

Lucien nodded. "All right, I'll need to see that material, of course, but I still have one or two other concerns. For one thing, the plan needs a movie theater.''

"We thought of that,'' Pete said, "but there are already two downtown.''

"How modern are they? How many screens have stadium seating? Can the market support a third?''

"I'll find out. What else?''

"I think you're off base on condominium and apartment space. A definite move is underway in this country to taking residence closer to one's work. This market is prime for that, but you don't have enough affordable units. Some of those large, expensive spaces need to be broken into smaller, less expensive ones.''

Avis gradually let out her breath. It seemed that Lucien was serious about the project. Whatever else he was, he was a conscientious businessman.

Pete nodded in reply to Luc's suggestion. "Avis proposed that very thing to the architect, and she had a few other ideas that he really liked, too, a supermarket, for one, and a rooftop swimming pool and garden for another.''

Lucien looked at her with a touch of surprise. "Excellent. I'd envisioned the pool but didn't think of the supermarket, frankly.''

In spite of her personal disquiet Avis felt a spurt of pride. "Downtown doesn't have a grocery market, and now that living space is being developed here, it really needs one, but to get the most out of it, the supermarket needs to be at front street level with its own parking. Unfortunately that means acquiring the lot next door, which contains a small barbecue restaurant. It can be done reasonably if we're quick and quiet, but with parking in the area at a premium, I think we should consider building a parking garage on at least part of that space."

"Phase Four," Pete interjected, "if we decide to go that way."

Luc nodded thoughtfully, his eyes never leaving Avis. "I'll need surveys, plats, a complete prospectus, and if, as you say, this has to be done quickly and quietly, then I need them as soon as possible."

"We're revising our prospectus now," Pete said eagerly.

"Not we," Luc said. Sitting back and crossing his legs, he finally addressed Pete. "I find that too many hands actually slow the work at times. You know the old saying, too many cooks and what have you. I think it's best if I work with Avis on this. She seems to have the most innovative ideas."

"But this is Pete's project," Avis protested instantly. "He was working this deal long before he and I entered into partnership. He found the architect. He put together the initial investments."

"That's true," Pete confirmed. "Avis didn't even really want to be involved. I had to talk her into it."

"Good thing you did," Luc told him calmly, "because I'm afraid that is the only non-negotiable point for me. Either I work with Avis on this or I don't work on this at all, and that, of course, means Corydon doesn't get involved.''

"Now wait just a minute!" Avis exclaimed. "Pete has a vested interest in this deal."

"*I* have the money," Lucien pointed out smoothly. "It's very simple. I work with you or I take my money and I go."

"That's not fair."

"Thirty million dollars," he said flatly, "means that I get to decide what's fair and what isn't in this situation."

Avis felt her temper rise. "This is ridiculous."

"That's not the word I'd use," Pete muttered, glaring at Luc.

"Use any word you like," Luc told him, returning that glare.

For a long moment, silence reigned, then Pete looked from Luc to Avis and back again before abruptly shoving back his chair. "Hey. You want to work with Avis, that's fine."

"Pete, this is your project!" she protested.

"This is about money, Avis, not ego. If he prefers to deal with you, I'm cool with it." He looked at Lucien, adding, "Besides, we all know I'll be involved every step of the way, just behind the scenes." He rose and dropped his napkin in his chair seat.

"I don't like this," she told him, voice shaking with repressed anger and dismay.

He moved to her side, dropped a hand on her shoulder and bent low to speak into her ear. "You brought him here, honey. You're the draw; I can see that. Now you do what you do best and make me proud.''

"Pete," she pleaded.

"You can handle him," he said. Then he straightened and walked around her chair to face Lucien Tyrone. He didn't offer Lucien his hand, and though Luc rose, he didn't offer his, either.

"I expect you to make me lots of money, Mr. Tyrone," Pete said, an edge of warning in his voice, "you and my girl here."

Luc stiffened. "That's *one* of the things I do best, Mr. Coeli. I think perhaps Avis could attest to some of my other talents."

Avis gasped and grit her teeth as the two men stood there, staring one another down. Then Pete turned, looked at her, and walked away.

She dropped her gaze to her hands, mortified and struggling to control her temper. Lucien resumed his seat. For a long moment, she did not trust herself to speak, and he seemed to feel no need to do so. Then, suddenly, she couldn't stop herself. "How dare you! Pete is my partner. You don't have any right to cut him out of this project. And you certainly don't have the right to make that kind of innuendo in front of him."

"I'm not much concerned with rights just now."

"No, all you care about is getting what you want!"

He smiled grimly at that. "But unlike most of the world, I make no apologies for it."

"Well, just like everyone else, you can't always have what you want. That's life."

"True. You, for instance, did not get rid of me as easily as you wanted."

"And that's what this is really about, isn't it?" she hissed, remembering that they were in a public place.

Instead of answering her, he asked his own question. "Are you his girl, Avis?"

She squelched a tiny, irritating thrill at the thought that he might really care and turned up her nose. "That's none of your business."

"Are you Pete Coeli's girl?" he demanded in a low, tight voice. "Or is that something he wants and can't have?" As heat surged into her cheeks, he seemed to reach his own conclusion. "Is that a game you play, Avis? Do you make men want you and then hold back?"

"Don't be ridiculous."

"You didn't hold back very much with me," Lucien went on, "but it was enough to make me crazy." She looked up in horrified surprise at that. "How much have you held back with Coeli?" he demanded.

"Pete is my partner!" she shouted, and immediately clapped a hand over her mouth, dropping her gaze. When she looked up a moment later, she was shocked to find Lucien as blazingly angry as she was.

A muscle quivered in the hollow of his jaw. "You didn't answer the question."

"It doesn't deserve an answer."

"But will have one, nonetheless."

This rigid, commanding Lucien was someone she didn't know, but she realized that the only way to satisfy him was to give him what he wanted, which was simple enough. "It was just a figure of speech.

I'm not Pete Coeli's girl in any romantic sense of the word. I'm his business partner. That's all.''

''But he would like it to be more.''

She didn't refute that. Let him infer what he would. ''Now you have to answer a question for me. Are you in this deal or not?''

Lucien crossed his legs, seeming very relaxed suddenly, and brushed the backs of his fingers across his thigh. ''That depends.''

''On what?''

''On you.''

She had been very much afraid he was going to say that, and now that he had, she could do nothing but stare at him in dismay.

He suddenly leaned forward again. ''Did you really think you could just walk away?'' he demanded, tight-lipped, revealing the depth and breadth of the pride that had brought him here. For one insane moment, she hoped that it might be more, but then she closed her heart against the possibility that he might truly care for her as a person, a whole woman. What difference did it make? Ken had cared, after all, and his caring had trapped her.

''Yes,'' she said, suddenly desperate to get away. Shooting to her feet, she picked up her handbag from the corner of the table and slapped it beneath her arm. ''And I still think I can.'' With that she turned and stalked out of the restaurant.

Luc clamped his jaw and fisted both hands, aware that he'd handled her badly. That feminine, soft-spoken exterior was built around a backbone of pure

steel, as he knew only too well. Forcing the issue
would never succeed with Avis. One needed charm
and careful, thoughtful negotiation with such a
woman, and even then it would be a real fight. Adept
in the art of submission, she played her implacable
will like an ace up her sleeve, giving in and giving
in and giving in until one finally noticed that she
hadn't really given what was most desired at all—
and never would if pressed. Having learned that les-
son in London, he'd meant to entice, even to entrap
if necessary; instead he had confronted her with his
wounded pride, and as before she had simply walked
away.

Well, he wasn't about to put up with that, not after
weeks of designing his battle plans and marshaling
his forces. Hours and hours of research had been involved. Favors had been called in. Friends had been
importuned, not to mention the millions of dollars
used to purchase Corydon and set up its reserves. Yet,
the campaign had barely begun, and she thought to
route him with retreat. As if she could run fast and
far enough to leave him behind her. He hadn't
thought her so foolish—or himself so angry, angry
enough to frighten her away again, and she was
afraid. He had seen it in her eyes. But of what? Another mystery to be unraveled.

Sighing, he signaled the waiter. While he was settling the bill, he had his car brought around. It waited
for him when he walked out of the restaurant, the
valet standing stiffly by the open door. Lucien dis-
liked hired limos and drivers, finding it much more
expedient to own not only the automobile but the

OFFICIAL OPINION POLL

ANSWER 3 QUESTIONS AND WE'LL SEND YOU
2 FREE BOOKS AND A FREE GIFT!

0074823 |||||||||||| ||||||| |||||||| FREE GIFT CLAIM # 3953

YOUR OPINION COUNTS!

Please check TRUE or FALSE below to express your opinion about the following statements:

Q1 Do you believe in "true love"?

"TRUE LOVE HAPPENS ONLY ONCE IN A LIFETIME."
○ TRUE
○ FALSE

Q2 Do you think marriage has any value in today's world?

"YOU CAN BE TOTALLY COMMITTED TO SOMEONE WITHOUT BEING MARRIED."
○ TRUE
○ FALSE

Q3 What kind of books do you enjoy?

"A GREAT NOVEL MUST HAVE A HAPPY ENDING."
○ TRUE
○ FALSE

YES, I have scratched the area below.

Please send me the 2 FREE BOOKS and FREE GIFT for which I qualify. I understand I am under no obligation to purchase any books, as explained on the back of this card.

335 SDL DZ32   235 SDL DZ4H

FIRST NAME   LAST NAME

(S-SE-03/04)

ADDRESS

APT.#   CITY

www.eHarlequin.com

STATE/PROV.   ZIP/POSTAL CODE

The Silhouette Reader Service™—Here's How It Works:

Accepting your 2 free books and gift places you under no obligation to buy anything. You may keep the books and gift and return the shipping statement marked "cancel." If you do not cancel, about a month later we'll send you 6 additional books and bill you just $3.99 each in the U.S., or $4.74 each in Canada, plus 25¢ shipping & handling per book and applicable taxes if any.* That's the complete price and — compared to cover prices of $4.75 each in the U.S. and $5.75 each in Canada — it's quite a bargain! You may cancel at any time, but if you choose to continue, every month we'll send you 6 more books, which you may either purchase at the discount price or return to us and cancel your subscription.

*Terms and prices subject to change without notice. Sales tax applicable in N.Y. Canadian residents will be charged applicable provincial taxes and GST.

If offer card is missing write to: Silhouette Reader Service, 3010 Walden Ave., P.O. Box 1867, Buffalo NY 14240-1867

BUSINESS REPLY MAIL

FIRST-CLASS MAIL   PERMIT NO. 717-003   BUFFALO, NY

POSTAGE WILL BE PAID BY ADDRESSEE

SILHOUETTE READER SERVICE
3010 WALDEN AVE
PO BOX 1867
BUFFALO NY 14240-9952

NO POSTAGE
NECESSARY
IF MAILED
IN THE
UNITED STATES

loyalties of the driver, as well. Some things, however, could not be avoided, and he was resigned to the situation, at least in the short term. With resignation came the intention that she would appreciate the many compromises he had made and the trouble to which he had gone on her behalf. Eventually.

Giving the driver her address, he sat back and prepared himself for what he expected to be a relatively long trip. The driver knew his way around, however, and didn't quail at speed limits. The limo eased into the northern outskirts of the tiny city of Puma Springs little more than half an hour after blowing past those on the southern edge of Fort Worth. Luc looked around him with interest as the driver consulted his GPS unit and carefully negotiated the broad streets.

Another six or seven minutes passed before the limo pulled into the very narrow drive of a partial two-story, clapboard and brick veneer house with a single-bay front-entry garage. The siding had been painted the same cheery yellow as the buttercups that dotted the flowerbeds in front of the low, boxy shrubs bordering the house and walkway. The rich, deep green of the shrubs repeated on the rooftops and paneled front door, which was flanked by large terra cotta pots filled with purple pansies. The faux shutters that trimmed the windows and the garage door added a measure of pristine white.

Luc saw a modest but well-kept place with a neatly mown lawn and edging of the same dark red brick as the veneer, all very neat, almost regimental, except for the pansies and the weeping willow tree swaying seductively in the far front corner of the yard. That tree and the flowerpots were the only things about the place that put him in mind of Avis. The rest seemed the product of an altogether different hand.

He wanted to tell the driver that he wouldn't be needing him anymore that night, but for the first time within easy memory, Lucien Tyrone wasn't sure that he could convince the lady that he should stay. "Wait here," he finally instructed, the words leaving the taste of ash in his mouth as he let himself out of the back seat.

"Yes, sir."

Mentally girding himself for battle, Lucien walked up the cracked, slightly sloping front drive in his Italian leather shoes, climbed the steps to the shrub-hemmed stoop, tugged at the French cuffs of his pale-blue dress shirt, eased the muscles across his shoulders by craning his neck slightly and reached for the doorbell.

Avis paced the bedroom floor in her stocking feet, still dressed except for her shoes. The doorbell brought her to a halt. Angry, worried and fearful all at once, she'd searched for some way out of this mess, asking herself over and over what she could do. TexBank was almost assuredly a bust now that she'd walked away from the thirty million dollars Lucien had been prepared to invest, but she hadn't been able to stop herself. How dare Lucien think he could just waltz into her life again any time it pleased him? Because he was Lucien Tyrone, of course, rich as Croesus and used to getting whatever he wanted whenever he wanted it. Well, not this time.

But poor Pete. She put a hand to her head, wondering if Pete could ever forgive her. How was she going to explain? She'd have to tell him about London, about her affair with Lucien. Would he hate her, she wondered, or just be sad and disappointed? She couldn't decide which would be worse. And it was all Lucien Tyrone's fault! The audacity and sheer arrogance of the man simply astounded. Oh, why couldn't he have stayed away and let her be?

The doorbell rang again, and she jumped, knowing perfectly well who was ringing it. A bolt of terror shot through her, canceled by another of shameful delight. The bell began chiming repeatedly, insistently. Suspecting that it could go on all night, she yielded to the inevitable and descended the stairs. In the foyer, she called out that she was coming, then took a moment to steel herself as the ringing stopped. Finally, she opened the door and folded her arms, striving for a nonchalance she did not feel.

"I never figured you for a stalker, Lucien."

He smiled apologetically, beseechingly, once again the Lucien she had known so well in London. "If being captivated qualifies me as a stalker, then I plead guilty to all charges."

She frowned, despite a pronounced flutter inside her chest, unwilling to be charmed. "This is pointless, you know."

"Then what can it hurt to let me come in?"

When he put it that way, she could hardly refuse. Besides, this was best settled in private, not in some restaurant or even on her doorstep. She turned aside, and he entered the foyer, craning his head curiously.

She would not let herself think how far below his usual standards her little house fell. Funny, it had not seemed lacking in any way before she had met him.

"Can we sit?" he asked, turning to her.

She inclined her head and led the way into the open living area, feeling brittle. A club chair sat at an angle to the end of the matching sofa, both pieces upholstered in buff suede and accented with neat, tailored pillows sporting a rose tapestry cover. She waved a hand, and he positioned himself in front of the chair, but then he stood looking at her until she crossed to the fireplace and sat gingerly on the painted brick hearth. An arched brow seemed to say that he found her attempt to keep distance between them amusing.

Tugging at his pants legs, he sat. For a long moment, he simply stared at her, a lovely, masculine apparition from her past, where he should have stayed. Finally, he cleared his throat.

"I've missed you."

A frisson of hot delight swept through her, but she denied it with a turn of her head. "Oh, please. We both know why you're here."

"I'm here," he said firmly, "because I've missed you."

She found herself on her feet again. "I don't like games, Lucien."

"Well, that makes two of us. Why don't you stop pretending that you aren't glad to see me so we can discuss this like adults?"

"You think I'm pretending?" she asked incredulously. "For the record, I don't want you here, Lucien. I want you to leave. Go away and take your money and your schemes with you.''

His expression hardened, giving his face a chiseled appearance, and his hands gripped the rolled ends of the arms of the chair. ''Your partner might have something to say about that.''

She turned away, hugging herself. ''Pete will understand.''

''Will he?'' She heard him come to his feet but barely had time to turn to face him before he was on her, his big hands capturing her shoulders. ''Will he understand when he hears how easily and how often you came to my bed? Considering how he feels about you, I think he'll understand why I am here, but I also think he'll be hurt, and we aren't talking about TexBank.''

True. All true. She imagined Pete's disappointed face and closed her eyes, desperation clawing through her. ''Oh, please,'' she whispered. ''For the love of God, please!''

He shook her, just once, insisting that she open her eyes. ''How dare you bring up love?'' he demanded roughly. ''You walked away from it!''

Her eyes snapped wide. Walked away from love? From *love?* Horror rolled through her, and something else, a longing so sharp and dangerous that it made her cry out. Then his arms were around her, and his mouth was on hers. Gladness rushed through her in a sickening wave of giddiness, and any hope of resistance washed away with the tide.

Chapter Nine

Home. Being in his arms again was like going home at last after a long and tiring journey, and while one part of her reeled in horror, the rest simply couldn't get enough.

Her hands closed in the fabric of his suit coat, her mouth opening for the ardent invasion of his tongue. She had tried so hard to forget how sweet that tongue was, how it played in all the secret recesses of which she herself was barely aware, evoking tremors and little floods of heat. Her body reveled in its contact with his, thigh to thigh, belly to belly, breasts to chest, feet interlaced, arms entwined. Mouth to mouth. Ah, why did it feel like belonging?

His hands rose to her hair, plucking and tugging at pins and clips until his fingers could slide against her scalp, tilting her head just so in order to accommodate the deeper plunge of his tongue, and all the while, she clutched at him, bringing her elbows close to her body in order to bring her body harder against his. She felt the bulge of his desire against her, every heavenly inch of it, and her body wept for more.

Increasingly frantic, she forgot to be frightened, forgot everything but the joy of being filled by him, connected, one. She tried to wrap her arms around his neck, but his hands got in the way. He dropped them to her waist, pulling her tighter as he tilted his hips against her. Frustration howled. She went up on tiptoe, twined her leg about his, the slit in her dress pulling wide, and found a sweet pressure that only made her want more.

He rocked his hips, rubbing against her, his hands cupping her bottom now and holding her in place as his mouth plundered hers with tongue and teeth and lips. Gripping his hair, she mindlessly sought relief by grinding against him everywhere she could manage. A spasm of sensation rippled upward, and her body exulted, certain now that it was going to get where and what it wanted. Nirvana beckoned. Ecstasy hovered. His hand slid between them, cupped her breast, and it was all she could do not to melt and ruin that delightful friction. Then his hand moved awkwardly to the center of her chest and pushed just hard enough to break the kiss.

She opened her eyes—When had she closed them?—and felt the room spin. Blinking, she tried to adjust, confused by that hand on her chest holding her away from him and the one on her bottom locking her close. Then he rasped, "Where is your bed-room?"

She twisted toward the stairs, and as they wavered into focus, she suddenly realized what she was doing. *So do it,* she told herself. *You've done it before.* But this time it would be different. If she took him to her bed like this, she would never again own herself, never again have her own life to live in her own way. There were no finite boundaries this time, no escape clauses, no easy exits. This time she would be trapped as surely as ever Kenneth had trapped her.

With a cry, she wrenched free of him, stumbling in her bare feet across the carpet. The skirt of her beloved sapphire dress ripped above the slit almost to the waist, shredding the delicate fabric.

He stretched out a hand to her, concern knitting his brow. "Avis?"

She drew back, chest heaving. "No!"

He tilted his head, looking like a curious puppy, charmingly confused. His gaze slid to the tear in her dress. "I'll buy you another," he said soothingly.

She recoiled. He might as well have said that he'd lock her in a closet and throw away the key. "I-I want you to leave."

He chuckled. "Darling, I know the difference be-tween hello and good-bye. That was a welcome kiss."

The color drained from her face. "Get out of my house!"

Lucien stared. Then he shook his head, his face hardening into that sculpted mask again. "You try my patience." He shoved both hands through his hair, which she had disarranged with hers. "You tell me, 'Go!' But your body pleads, 'Stay!' I want to know what your heart says. Tell me that, if you can!"

Anger unlike anything she had felt before, more intense than any she had ever allowed herself, boiled up into her throat. "How dare you? How dare you! Do you think I'm stupid enough to listen to my heart? I'm not twenty years old anymore! I'm not a thing you can own! I'm not just some pretty convenience you can pick up on a whim. I'm a human being. I have my own life, my own thoughts, my own goals! I won't let you put me back into a box of obligation and…" She put her hand over her mouth, aware that she was raving. He stared at her in stunned silence until she twisted away in shame. "Please," she whispered, "just go."

For a long, torturous moment, nothing. Then he cleared his throat. "All right."

She looked at him with surprised hope. A muscle twitched in the hollow of his jaw. His fisted hands relaxed. He smoothed his tie, rotating his shoulders.

"I'll go," he said calmly, "for now. But I'll be back in a week. One week."

Her heart thudded. "D-don't."

He suddenly pointed a finger at her. "We are in business together. I expect the last parcel to be purchased and the prospectus brought up to speed by the time I get back here."

She blinked. "You're staying with the TexBank deal?"

"I'm not stupid, Avis," he said imperiously. "It's

a good project. If it wasn't, I'd have found another way.''

"Another way?" she echoed uncertainly.

He shrugged that aside as inconsequential. "Corydon funds will go into a special account for the time being. Update the prospectus. Buy the parcel. Within the week.''

She gulped. "The parcel. Y-you mean the lot next to the bank building.''

"With the restaurant," he confirmed, tugging at his cuffs. "You might consider offering them space inside the mall as an incentive.''

She nodded and mumbled, "That might work to our advantage, but it also means revealing our plans. What about keeping things quiet?''

He dismissed that with an impatient wave of one hand. "We don't want things quiet. We want all the buzz we can generate.''

"But we haven't even purchased the bank tower yet.''

"Oh, but we have.''

She felt a chill rush over her. "You mean that *you* have." He just looked at her. "My God! And Pete doesn't have a clue.''

Lucien grimaced. "I'm not cutting out anyone. The thing needed to be done quickly to get the best price. You'll have control of the second parcel, and once the word is out on the streets, we'll have tenants lining up outside our door, but we have to act *now*." He pointed his finger at her again. "*You* have to act now. Understand?''

She understood, all right. She understood that

Pete's dreams and plans rode completely on her shoulders. Well, Pete was going to get his TexBank deal. All she was going to get out of it was a lousy week's reprieve. So be it. In a week, Lucien Tyrone was going to find a changed woman on his hands, a woman in control, in command of her emotions and impulses. She nodded and lifted her chin. ''One week,'' she confirmed reluctantly.

Lucien smiled. Something soft and dangerous glittered in his dark eyes. He was the predator again, patiently stalking his prey. Then he spun on his heel and strode into the foyer. She listened to his footsteps as he crossed the floor. The door opened and closed. Footsteps pattered and shushed on concrete. A car engine rumbled. Another door thumped mutedly. Tires crunched on the drive. Then only the rumble remained, fading gradually into silence.

She sank down onto the floor, gasping with relief. And worry.

''The man is wealthy beyond belief,'' Pete said, bending over the paper he'd just placed on her desk blotter. ''A billionaire, right up there with Gates and Onassis! He has a reputation for being ruthless in business, but his judgment is renowned. One word from him and we're made, kiddo.''

Avis shook her head. She'd known that he was wealthy, of course, but she'd never imagined that he could be one of the world's richest men! What on earth did a man like that want with her? Pete mistook her reaction for disbelief.

''I'm telling you, Avis, the man is Midas.'' He

perched on the edge of her desk. "According to my sources, his father left him well off, but Luc has more than quadrupled his inheritance since then. His personal life is pretty much a mystery since his wife died. Apparently he likes to keep a low profile, but they say that, all things considered, he's real down to earth."

Avis snorted at that, but then she had to rethink. He'd flown commercial, after all, and while his London townhouse was lovely and opulent, it wasn't a mansion set in the middle of a hundred acres and sealed off by an impregnable wall. She bit her lip, more confused than ever. Had he really implied that he was in love with her? Or was that just something he used to get his way? She shivered, wondering which conclusion would be worse. "I don't like this."

Pete threw up his arms. "What's not to like? Lucien Tyrone has put us on the map, sweetheart. TexBank is going to succeed like magic!"

"But even at that it's small potatoes to a man like him," she argued.

"So? A good deal is still a good deal. Maybe he's looking for a toehold in the DFW market and the fact that he met you in England tipped the scales in our favor. Did he really go sightseeing with you in London?"

She nodded distractedly. "Umm-hmm."

"There, see! Down to earth, just like I said. By the way, Cabot has increased his investment by sixty percent."

Avis's mouth fell open. Marshal Cabot was known

for his conservative investment practices. "That means he's more than doubled his bank's investment in the project!"

"Actually," Pete informed her with a smirk, "he matched the bank's investment with one of his own and then went ten percent better."

"Good grief! If this keeps up we can do it without Lucien!" she exclaimed hopefully. Then she remembered that Lucien actually owned the property now, a fact Pete still did not know.

Pete hopped onto his feet, chortling good-naturedly. "No way, sister. Without Lucien Tyrone, all we'd have from Cabot and everyone else is an iffy promise. I'm telling you, Avis, the day you bumped into the Greek Tycoon was the luckiest day of your life—and mine, too." With that he dropped a kiss on her cheek and headed for the door.

Avis felt a jolt of shock. "The Greek Tycoon," she muttered resentfully.

"That's what they call him on Wall Street," Pete called gaily as he swept through the door.

Avis sat stunned. Everyone knew about the Greek Tycoon. He was rumored to be one of the most ruthless corporate raiders in history. Hadn't she suspected from the beginning that Luc was involved in that sort of thing? He'd thrown her off with a dose of casual, charming honesty. Except that he hadn't said who he really was. Okay, so he hadn't exactly lied, either. So what?

Avis put a hand to her head. The world had turned upside down. Pete seemed distant, cheery but distant—and resigned, as if he'd yielded the field where she was concerned. She felt trapped, and she'd sworn to herself that she would never feel this way again. It wasn't scandal or infirmity and illness that held her this time. Oh, no. It was the hopes and purposes of two very different men. She couldn't help resenting both of them.

The transaction went like clockwork. The contracts between C&L and Corydon were not even signed yet, but the word was out on the street that Lucien Tyrone was in on the TexBank deal, and that was good enough. The owners of the BBQ joint that occupied the lot next to the damaged TexBank building didn't even know who Lucien Tyrone was, but they were anxious to do business with the infamous Greek Tycoon. Avis dutifully pointed out that they were selling to C&L I&D, but their accountant had told them that the Greek-American billionaire was involved, and that seemed to override any other details. It also doubled the price of the property, even with the incentive of mall space for a carry-out business thrown in.

Avis inked the deal anyway, thinking that if it sank the project, that might be for the best, after all. The worst that could happen was that Luc would have to buy out C&I's interest to make the deal work the way he wanted it to. Or he could just scuttle the whole project. But no, he was too good a businessman for that. Still, she didn't trust Lucien Tyrone, and she was dismayed that Pete did. When he came waltzing into her office with the contracts the very day after they'd purchased the restaurant lot, two attorneys and Candy in tow, she fought to keep her bitterness from showing.

"Put your pretty little name on the dotted line, darlin', and let's celebrate!" Pete crowed. Candy carried a bottle of champagne by the neck and a stack of plastic tumblers.

Avis stared at the sheaf of papers that Pete plunked down in front of her, recognizing the names of their company and Corydon, Inc. She darted a glance at their attorney, a tall, muscular young man with the unfortunate name of Hanson Biggot and more hair sticking out of his ears than on the top of his head. Corydon's rep was an urbane, middle-aged gentleman of impeccable stature and old money sensibility by the name of Robert Sanford.

"Are you sure this is wise?" she asked Pete, but it was Biggot who answered her.

"It's a fair contract, Ms. Lorimer. I went over it with a fine-tooth comb."

"I'm sure you did, Mr., er, but, ah…" She glanced at Pete, who slid his hands into his pockets and shrugged.

"But Corydon owns the TexBank building," Pete said affably. "It was a good move on Tyrone's part. Now we're buying in with the second parcel."

"We're not in control, Pete."

"We never were. It's true that I envisioned a deal with a lot of little partners that would give us control, but we spun our wheels for two years with that plan. The point is, it's still *our* plan, and we're going to make so much off this that next time we'll be driving the bus."

Sanford chuckled and placed his briefcase on her desk. "Well put."

Pete rocked back on his heels. "I had the sweet job of turning down money this morning. Can you get over that? Winston Bank wants a piece of us now, and they've turned down every proposal I've ever put to them. Serves 'em right, I say." He plucked a pen from his shirt pocket and offered it to her, adding, "You first, partner. If it weren't for you, old Tyrone would never have looked our way."

"Is that so?" Sanford mused.

Avis gingerly took the pen as Biggot came to stand beside her and flipped the pages to the right place. Lucien's signature and one other were already on the paper. She took a deep breath.

"Sure is," Pete answered Sanford proudly. "Avis met Tyrone in London months ago."

For Pete, she told herself, putting aside her resentment, and began writing.

"Must've made some impression," Candy said, popping the cork on the champagne bottle. Avis flinched, flubbing her signature.

"Well, she would, wouldn't she?" Pete said, making Avis cringe. "Lucien Tyrone. I knew there was a reason she was immune to my good looks," he teased, and Avis could gladly have slunk under the desk to hide.

"Bet old Tyrone didn't know what hit him," Biggot put in. "Texas women are just better looking than average, don't you think?" Candy beamed while Avis felt her face heat with color.

"Why, thank you, Mr. Biggot," the secretary said with a wide grin.

Avis scribbled her name again as the young attorney indicated and shoved away the papers. Candy was busy pouring champagne and making a mess of everything. She sat a glass in front of Avis and shoved another at Sanford who demurred and came away with the glass in hand anyway. Biggot accepted his eagerly while Pete signed his own name with bold slashes of the pen. Sanford divested himself of the bubbly in order to sign as witness to the event, followed by Biggot, who managed one-handed. Then Candy proposed a toast.

"Here's to success, y'all, and a big fat raise in my paycheck."

Everyone laughed but Avis, who barely managed a sip while the others were chugging theirs and talking. Sanford emptied his glass but refused another. Candy had already refilled her own and sloshed golden liquid on Avis's desk blotter while refilling Biggot's. Pete, meanwhile, smiled at his empty tumbler and cast a warm look on Avis.

"We're on our way, kid."

She couldn't even muster a smile for him, but she didn't have to. Everyone else was smiling and laughing and chatting as if it was a real party. Why did she feel that the only place she was on her way to was the end of the world?

The end of the world arrived at 11:45 p.m. The end of the world apparently involved luggage. Lucien shoved a heavy tanned leather garment bag into the foyer and dropped a matching briefcase on top of it. "I usually travel light."

"You never heard of wheels?"

He shrugged, and she rolled her eyes. Of course he hadn't bothered to buy wheeled luggage. Why should he when someone else always carried it for him? She stepped around the bags in question to peer out the door for whoever had carried them this far. He could just carry them right back again to wherever they came from. Except that he was nonexistent. She caught the glow of red taillights as a car braked before turning right at the corner. Lucien had had himself dropped off at her house. With his luggage!

She slammed the door. "What do you think you're doing?"

"It's reciprocity," he said with a cheeky grin. "You stayed with me in England."

"At your invitation!"

"Exactly."

She folded her arms. "You can't stay here."

"I have to stay somewhere until I can set up a place of my own."

"Does the word *hotel* mean anything to you?"

"I hate hotels."

"Oh, well."

"Why do you think I own so many homes?"

"Because you can?"

"Because I hate hotels. Besides, there isn't a hotel in Fort Worth where I can stay."

"Don't give me that."

"I tried," he insisted. "I've just come from a hotel."

"Not up to your standards?" She could barely keep the sneer out of her voice.

"The accommodations were acceptable," he said. "The security was not."

"Security? Like this place is Fort Knox."

"I had sixteen voice mails and a dozen handwritten notes waiting for me when I checked in. The staff there had never heard of the concept of discretion. It was blazoned across the marquee out front. Welcome, Mr. Tyrone!" He made a gesture with one hand and rattled off something in Greek. "The lobby would have been packed with gawkers by morning."

She had to admit that he had a point. They'd been fielding calls at their office for two days, reporters wanting interviews with the Greek Tycoon, bankers begging for introductions, women asking where he was going to be for lunch. But none of that mattered. He simply could not stay here. "You brought it on yourself. There are other hotels, more discreet ones, I'm sure."

"In Dallas," he said pointedly. "I don't think that's very politic, do you?" She frowned. The two cities were often in a state of rivalry. It wouldn't look too good for Fort Worth's business community if their bright new star was known to be staying in Dallas. "Besides," he went on, "it's too far away. I'm a busy man, and we have work to do."

It was on the tip of her tongue to tell him to go stay with Pete, but she could just imagine where that would lead. She could almost hear the conversation now.

She fell right into my arms. Long baths together in

my London townhouse. Making love on a bed older than most nations, on the floor in front of the fireplace, in her dressing room, in my dressing room, the back of a limo...

No wonder I couldn't get to first base. Can't compete with that.

She definitely didn't want him to stay at Pete's. Closing her eyes, she accepted the inevitable.

"This is not London," she said waspishly. "I don't have servants, and I don't cook. Much. There is no elevator. The bathroom is small, and the hot water comes out of a single tank. Use it all, and I'll kick your billionaire butt to the curb."

He grinned. "Where's your guest room? Or am I welcome in the master?"

She eyed him sternly. "The guest room is beneath the stairs, second door to your right. The first is the bath. No, it does not connect. Be sure you're decent when you come and go."

He hoisted his bags. "So this is that Southern hospitality I've heard so much about."

"It's all of it you're going to get. And temporary. Very temporary."

His dark eyes twinkled. "We'll see about that." He lumbered down the hall, dragging his luggage. She smugly bet herself that wheels would be on the agenda quite soon.

"Reciprocity my Aunt Fanny," she grumbled, but then she stiffened her spine. No more sweet, soft-spoken Avis, going along to get along. Give that man an inch, and he'd take *two* miles. And figure he was entitled to them. Well, he was not entitled to her, and the sooner he got that straight, the better. Now all she had to do was hold firm until then.

Why, she wondered, did that feel akin to filling the Grand Canyon with a teaspoon?

Chapter Ten

"I'm leaving for the office in ten minutes," she shouted through the bedroom door. "If you expect to go with me, you'd better shake a leg. I won't wait."

After a sleepless night, she'd risen early, dressed and drunk half a pot of coffee before pounding on the guest-room door. She could hear him grumbling behind that door now, then suddenly he yanked it open, wearing nothing more than hastily donned silk pajama bottoms. The man slept naked, as she well knew. He looked and smelled as inviting as a warm, rumpled bed, with his ash-blond hair adorably mussed, lids drooping over his exotic eyes and the shadow of a morning beard on his jaws.

"Am I not allowed even a single cup of coffee for breakfast?" he snapped. "Back in London, I gave you breakfast in bed nearly every morning, if you recall, not to mention—''

''I'll pour the coffee,'' she interrupted, not caring to recall what amenities he'd provided nearly every morning back in London. ''You get dressed, or I swear I'll leave without you.''

''It's not nice to swear,'' he groused as she strode away.

She did not deign to reply, but once she was a safe distance away she did let loose the grin tweaking the corner of her mouth. Carrying coffee, she returned to his room a few minutes later, surprised to find him suited and combed but unshaven. Electric razor in hand, he tucked his briefcase beneath one arm and reached for the coffee mug, crowding the doorway impatiently.

''Well, are you in a hurry or not?''

She spun on her heel and led him back through the house to the kitchen, where she picked up her purse from the counter. He slurped the hot brew as they moved to the door that led through the utility room to the garage. She ignored him and made for the car. After unlocking the driver's door, she dropped down behind the steering wheel. He hastily pulled the utility room door closed, pocketed the shaver and walked around behind the coupe to the passenger side. She let him wait while she stowed her purse, buckled her seat belt, started the car engine and opened the garage bay with the punch of a button. Only then did she unlock his door. He shot her an accusing look as he eased down into the narrow seat, briefcase clutched awkwardly to his chest, coffee mug cradled in his hands.

She stalled for a moment, adjusting mirrors, before she said, ''It's a law in Texas that you have to wear your seat belt.''

''Oh.'' He balanced the cup in one hand, twisted and felt around with the other until he got hold of the end of the belt. It snapped back twice before he finally managed to get it buckled.

Turning her head so he wouldn't see her grin, she put the car into reverse and shot out of the garage. He exploded with something Greek, desperately grappling with the mug, over the rim of which sloshed hot coffee. It dripped onto his hands, knees and expensive leather briefcase.

''Oops,'' she said, not in the least sorry, and braked to a halt, sloshing him again.

He brushed at the black twill of his suit pants and sent her a sideways glare. ''You're very beautiful when you're vindictive.''

''Humph.'' She backed the car into the street and adjusted the transmission into the forward gear before inquiring sweetly, ''All set?''

He showed her his teeth. ''All set.''

As she navigated through the small town, he drank his coffee and looked around. ''Not much there,'' he commented as they left Puma Springs behind.

''Enough,'' she answered, intensely aware of him, the ease with which he held and carefully imbibed from his cup—and how his knees crowded the dashboard.

''At least you didn't intentionally ruin the coffee,''

he said cheerfully, draining the last drop. He looked around for something to do with the empty mug and finally found the cup holder beneath the dash before laboriously extracting the electric razor from his coat pocket. Getting at the mirror in the visor required him to tilt his head back while folding down the shade.

She took pity on him. "You can let the seat back by pressing the big button on the side there between the seat and the door."

"So that's where they've hidden it." He slid the seat all the way back, adjusted the visor so he could see himself in the mirror and began to remove his morning beard with the electric razor. Apparently he saw no reason to forego conversation in the process. "So you like small cars, eh?"

She spoke up to be heard over the buzz of the razor. "This is considered a mid-size."

"No? Really? Huh." He finished shaving in silence, folded up the visor and stashed his razor in an outside pocket of his briefcase, which now rested comfortably between his feet, then settled back to enjoy the ride. "This is interesting country."

"Yeah, if you like grassy hills and a few stunted trees."

"It's very open. The sky seems rather, well, immediate. I quite like that."

"This is nothing. If you like open skies, you should see West Texas or the Panhandle. Flat as a pancake for as far as the eye can see, at least on the Llano Estacado."

"Staked plains," he translated, and she nodded, unsurprised that he knew Spanish.

"West of the Pecos you get into the tail end of the Rockies," she told him. "It's mostly desert, but pretty dramatic in its way."

"What do they do there?"

"Ranching mostly."

They turned onto the highway and joined a steady stream of traffic heading into the city. Within minutes empty fields and the occasional house gave way to the suburbs, which flanked the road with gasoline stations, convenience stores and other businesses, some prosperous-looking, some not. By the time they reached the outskirts of Fort Worth itself and turned east, traffic had congested considerably but not slowed down. They sped bumper-to-bumper ten miles per hour over the limit past a highway patrolman who didn't blink an eye.

"You do this every day?" he asked, sounding appalled.

"Lately, I do. Before TexBank took off I worked from home two days a week."

"Now that sounds like a very good idea," he said. "How well set up is your office there?"

"Well enough."

"Do you have video-conferencing capability?"

She looked at him. "We don't even have video-conferencing capability at the office."

"I'll have it installed," he decided, "both places."

"That won't be necessary."

"I find it convenient," he said, as if that settled it, which was probably the case.

She gritted her teeth and counted to ten.

No one said a word when she showed up at the

office with Lucien Tyrone in tow. In fact, they greeted him like a conquering hero, a very welcome one, much to her irritation. Pete even offered him his office.

"No, no, I'll squeeze in with Avis for the time being."

She rolled her eyes at that. "There's only one desk."

"We'll rent another," Luc said.

"There's room," Pete chimed in.

Luc just smiled.

Avis bit her tongue and gave in.

To her surprise, they actually got quite a lot accomplished that first day, though the morning was consumed with setting up Luc's work space. He didn't let that deter him, however, juggling two and sometimes three tasks at once. The phones rang constantly, including the one in his coat pocket, which he turned on only after nine o'clock. His assistant Lofton seemed to call every twenty minutes, and it began to grate on Avis's nerves.

"Shouldn't he be here anyway?" she asked after he interrupted their conference call with the architect for the fourth or fifth time. "What's the point in having an assistant if he's off somewhere else?"

"I do have other business interests," Lucien replied calmly. "Besides, I have *you* here."

Irritation flashed through her. "I am not your assistant."

"No," he agreed smoothly, "more like my good right arm in this."

What could she do but bite her tongue after that?

Lucien kept up a bruising pace that kept Avis running in and out of the office all day, ferrying papers and figures, while Pete showed in those whom Lucien deigned to see and stood between Luc and those he didn't. Candy fetched coffee and soft drinks and saw to it that lunch was catered right at Luc's newly delivered desk. At times, half a dozen people were in that office, installing, delivering, writing, fawning, talking over those already talking over the speaker phone. It was chaos, with Lucien at its center, as calm as the proverbial eye of the storm. When the last of the bedlamites had drifted away, Lucien pushed back his chair and rose to his feet.

"Time to call it a day." Avis nodded, too tired even to comment. He stuffed papers into his briefcase, seeming as energized as ever. "Want to stop off for dinner?" She managed to shake her head. "You need to eat."

"I intend to. But first I want a cup of tea and a long, hot bath. After that, I'll have a sandwich or something. Then I'm going to bed. Alone. You do as you please."

He chuckled. "I always do, and it pleases me to drive, provided you don't object."

She eyed him suspiciously as she dug out her keys. "Are you sure you know how?"

"I think I can manage."

She handed over the keys, secretly delighted that she didn't have to drive herself home tonight, but as they walked out into the hall and headed toward the elevators, she reminded herself that it wouldn't do to get too used to having Lucien Tyrone around.

* * *

Lucien listened to the water draining overhead and tried not to think of Avis getting out of the tub naked upstairs. It took every ounce of his self-discipline not to climb those stairs and slip into the room with her, but it was too soon for that. He'd flattered himself that she'd learned to trust him in London, but he knew now that was not the case, and he had to wonder just how bad her marriage had been to make her so wary. The whole thing was confusing, and not just where her feelings were concerned.

He'd told himself that he was coming after her as a matter of pride. He'd even scolded himself for it, wondered if his ego was getting out of hand, but all along he'd known that he would do what he had to do to make her understand that she was his. It was just that simple. And that complicated. He hadn't allowed himself to think that he might be in love with her, and he didn't intend to. He'd distracted himself, with business and now with one of his favorite but rarest indulgences, cooking.

Turning away from the fresh vegetables spread out atop the island work space, he bent to peek into the oven. Checking the casserole, he found the ''crust'' browning nicely. Too bad all she'd had in the pantry was bow-tie pasta instead of something substantial like penne. Her provisions, in fact, were woefully inadequate. Well, it couldn't be helped. He'd made do. He'd even managed a simple dessert.

He was tossing the salad when Avis finally wandered into the room, zipped from toe to chin in a fleece robe, her hair pulled into a bouncy ponytail atop her head. It was all he could do not to cup her freshly scrubbed face in his hands and kiss every square inch of it.

"What," she asked, parking her hands on her hips, "are you doing?"

He shrugged nonchalantly. "Making dinner."

She laughed. "Yeah, right."

"You don't think I can cook?"

"Why would you?"

"Because I like to putter around the kitchen almost as much as I like to eat." The timer buzzed just then, and he turned away, snatching up oven mitts to open the oven door. He lifted the dish from the hot oven-rack and turned with it to the island, where he set it on a trivet retrieved from the top of the refrigerator. "You don't seem to have any cream," he said, "so I used fat-free canned milk and threw in a couple of extra egg yolks, which reminds me. We should stop by the market tomorrow. And the liquor store. I'll make a list. We need eggs and cheese, bread... everything, really."

"I have cheese."

"I used it."

"But I had whole bricks of Romano *and* Parmesan."

"I used the Romano for the sauce. What's left of the Parmesan is on the table." He pointed, and she followed with her gaze to the table he had set earlier, using matching dishtowels in place of napkins. "The rest is in the crust."

Her eyes were wide when she turned back to him. "Mrs. Baldwin would be impressed."

"She'd be appalled. I used canned salmon. And you only have paper napkins."

Avis laughed, and he took that as a good sign. Lifting an arm, he ushered her to the table and watched her lower herself onto the chair. "Pour the wine while I bring the food to the table."

She reached for the bottle, grumbling, "You certainly have made yourself at home in my kitchen."

"It was that or call out for a pizza," he retorted, placing a salad plate in front of her.

"Have you ever actually called out for pizza?" she asked skeptically.

"Once or twice. Mine is better." He set a cruet of salad dressing on the table

She clucked her tongue. "I do have salad dressing."

"Bottled," he said dismissively.

"I like bottled."

"You'll like this better," he told her, "even though your olive oil is of an inferior grade."

She rolled her eyes and picked up her fork. Using matches he'd found in the cabinet, he lit the candles he'd brought in from the living room, then reached behind him for the light switch.

"What?" she quipped. "Afraid to let me actually see what I'm eating?"

He gave her a droll look. "You're eating salad. When you're done, I'll serve you a unique casserole baked with vegetables and salmon in a cream sauce."

She poured dressing on her lettuce and forked up a bite. She froze, and he smiled, knowing that the flavor had burst into her mouth in a perfect blend of sweet and sharp. She tilted her head appreciatively as she chewed. "You really made this?"

"I did."

She had a second helping of salad before she was ready for the casserole, but when he finally dished it up for her, she inhaled with obvious relish. He was pleased to see that the sauce had thickened appropriately and that the vegetables were as perfectly cooked as frozen could get.

"It's really best with fresh produce and real cream," he said, but the way she closed her eyes when she first tasted it pleased him immensely.

When she was done, she wiped up some of the sauce with her finger and carried it to her mouth. "You're just full of surprises, aren't you?"

"Mmm-hmm, including dessert, which needs to come out of the freezer." He rose to remove the dishes from the freezer and set them on the island to warm slightly. "At least you have a good blender," he told her. "I don't know how anyone gets by without a good blender."

She laughed long and hard at that for some reason, and though he couldn't imagine what was so funny about it, he smiled all the same, glad just to see her happy. She openly praised his frozen dessert, then watched attentively, sipping her wine, while he stashed the leftovers. Afterward, she insisted on cleaning up. "It's only fair. You cooked, after all."

He shrugged. "We can do it together. Most of it will go into the dishwasher. Keep your glass, though. I'd rather finish the wine than try to preserve it."

They made short work of the cleaning, him wash-

ing, her drying and putting away. Then as she started
the automatic washer, he poured them each another
glass of wine.

"Do you recycle?" he asked, holding up the empty
bottle.

She stared at him for a moment then shook her
head. "We don't have a program for it out here. I
had a friend once who hoped to change that, but after
his wife died, he sort of lost interest in the project."

"Tell me about that," he urged, leaning a hip
against the counter. He had learned much about her,
but not enough to satisfy his insatiable curiosity.

She twirled her glass by the stem. "He had all this
junk stacked up around his old house, and my friends,
Val and Sierra, and I, we heard that the new fire marshal was going to fine him for creating a fire hazard,
so we went to help clean it up. Turned out the fire
marshal was already there, not to fine him but to start
the clean-up himself. He and Val are married now,
by the way, and expecting a baby. His name's Ian
Keene. Anyway, that's when Edwin told us that he
and his wife had intended to recycle all that stuff but
that he didn't have the heart to carry on with the plan
once she passed. He died himself just a few weeks
after that, and then we found out that he was worth
millions and that he'd left it to the three of us
women."

"Edwin Searle," he said, remembering the name.
"Your guardian angel."

"Yes, my guardian angel."

"It sounds as though he loved his wife very
much."

She nodded and sighed. "That's one of the reasons we went to help him clean up the place that day. Edwin wasn't the easiest person to be nice to, you know? But his devotion to his wife's memory and his sister, who was sick, made us all think that his gruff exterior hid a very soft heart."

"And you were right."

"Yes, apparently we were."

He set aside his glass and reached for her. "I want a love like that, Avis," he said, realizing just then that it was so. "With you."

She, too, left her glass upon the counter, even as she shook her head. "Not with me, Luc. I don't know how to be the kind of woman who can be loved like that."

"But you do," he argued softly, brushing a tendril of hair back from her face. "You were that woman in London."

"No."

"Yes," he whispered. "If only for a time, you were that woman. Oh, yes." Then he bent his head and settled his mouth over hers.

She stood unresponsively within the loop of his arms for a moment before her hands drifted up to his shoulders and her mouth softened beneath his. He deepened the kiss by increments, gently drawing her closer, tilting her head with the pressure of his mouth. Relief and delight filled him. She still wanted him. Whatever she said, she still wanted him. Very soon, he was burning, desperate for more. He couldn't bring her close enough, couldn't draw enough from her mouth. Holding her trapped against the island with his hips and the strength of his kiss, he lifted trembling hands to the collar of her robe and un- zipped it far enough to get his hands inside. The weight of her breasts overflowing his palms was as welcome as water to a parched throat. But it was not enough. He laid his forehead against hers.

"Let's go upstairs. Let me show you that she's still here. That woman I loved in London is still here."

She pressed her hands over his, holding him to her, but she shook her head, tears rolling from beneath her closed eyelids. "I can't. I just can't."

"But why? Why can't we have what we had in London?"

She wrenched aside, clutching the front of her robe with both hands. "Because London is over, and there isn't anything else for us except business."

Frustration clawed at him, tying his groin in knots, raking his heart. "That doesn't make any sense. You want it as much as I do."

"I don't," she insisted. "I can't!" She stumbled out of the room in her bedroom slippers, and he let her go, afraid to do anything else, afraid that if he pushed her, she'd erect a wall so high and so wide that he'd never get around it.

He looked at their wineglasses, standing so close that not only did their sides touch, the feet of the pedestals overlapped. Picking them up, he drained them both, one after the other.

Chapter Eleven

"Mmm." Avis sighed, aware that she was dreaming. She'd promised herself that she would not, but the subconscious didn't listen to reason, and it was such a pleasant dream, not the disturbing tangle of arms and legs and heaving torsos that often woke her, embarrassed and steamy at the same time. This was a lovely, sweet illusion of affection, a nudge of the nose, a whisper of lips, the brush of fingertips across her brow, a warm breath in her ear and the delicious aroma of coffee. Was it London, then? Yes, of course, she was dreaming of London. For some reason she couldn't quite remember that was bad.

"Come on, sleepyhead. Your breakfast is getting cold."

"Mmm."

"That's it. Open those gorgeous eyes." She

opened her eyes, and found that she was not dreaming at all. Lucien's handsome face smiled down at her. "Good morning, beautiful."

She smiled, and then she realized that if she was not dreaming this could not be London, which meant that she was at home, and he... She frowned, found the covers and pulled them higher. "What are you doing in my bedroom?"

He rose from the edge of the bed and swept up the lap tray which she used for Kenneth once he could no longer sit in a chair. "It's only rice pudding with canned fruit, but it will fill the empty spaces and give you enough strength to accompany me grocery shopping before the workmen arrive."

"Workmen?"

"To install the video conferencing. I made the arrangements yesterday."

She sighed and pushed her hair back from her face. "I'd better get dressed then."

"No rush," he insisted, settling the tray over her lap. "We have time to eat."

The aroma of fresh coffee was too welcome to question. She reached for the nearest cup, brought it to her nose and inhaled before taking her first sip. Heaven. Drat the man, even his coffee was rich.

He settled onto the bed next to her in nothing more than those silk pajama pants and transferred a cup of coffee from the tray to her bedside table, then he helped himself to a bowl, spoon and paper napkin. She tried not to notice, to pretend that it was all very casual, but then she dipped a spoon into his rice pudding, and as the delicate concoction slid down her throat, bestowing bursts of vanilla and cinnamon on her unsuspecting taste buds, she couldn't help thinking that it wasn't fair. Why did he have to be handsome and romantic and sexy and rich *and* an excellent cook?

"This is a real treat," he said, waving around his spoon.

"Mmm, it's very good." She poked another bite into her mouth.

"No, I mean being here with you, having the time to spend in the kitchen, not worrying about hurting the cook's feelings or shocking the housemaid."

"You make having servants sound like a chore."

"Not a chore," he said, "but a responsibility. You know, someone else to consider. Every time I think about selling one of the houses I have to know that I'm thinking about putting someone out of work, several someones, usually."

She'd never thought of it like that. "Don't tell me you think of them all the way you do Mrs. Baldwin."

"Hardly. There is but one Hettie Baldwin. She practically raised me, you know. Until my father died, she was with us in San Francisco. Afterward, I let her go back to London, where Baldwin was waiting to sweep her off her feet."

"Let her?"

"I'd have kept her with us, but it was her wish to go." He slid a quick glance at Avis then back to his bowl, the contents of which were rapidly disappearing. "My mother is not always so easy to work for."

"Tell me about her."

"My mother? I love her, and she has been a godsend where my son Nicholas is concerned, but even my father likened her to a petite Mount Vesuvius.''

He loved his mother. Avis tried not to let that affect her too much, but it was difficult to harden one's heart against such a man. He looked at her for a moment as if he expected her to ask another question, but she found it safer not to. They finished eating in silence. She shoveled hers in with a purpose, then rose to toss a robe on over her cotton gown.

''Thank you. That was an excellent meal, but I'd rather you didn't make these gestures in the future.''

''Just trying to be a good guest,'' he said mildly.

She measured a doubtful look and sent it his way. ''Just leave the dishes. I'll take care of them.'' With that she quickly padded into the bathroom, considering that she had dismissed him, but when she emerged a few minutes later, he hadn't moved from her bed.

He lay with one arm folded comfortably beneath his head. The worst of it was that he looked right, as if he belonged there. She felt a twinge in her chest, and afterward, for some reason, she couldn't seem to breathe normally. He sat up, one leg crooked beneath him.

''I lied. I'm not trying to be a good guest. I don't even want to be your guest. I want to be your lover. It was so good, what we had in London.''

Memories suddenly assailed her, moments of pure abandonment, freedom, contentment. With him. Something inside her opened, like a flower to the morning sun.

He reached out a hand to her, and their palms con-

nected. She looked down in shock. Rising up on one
knee, he pulled her to him. His arms slid around her,
cradling her close, then he sank down and lay back,
taking her with him. He held her there against his
chest more with the force of his desire than the
strength of his arms. She could have pulled away,
could have been out of the room in a heartbeat. Instead she lay there, looking down into his dark, solemn eyes, feeling the thick, strong surge of her own
blood and the heat of his need.

"Make love with me," he whispered.

She stared at him helplessly before he tilted his
head and set his mouth to hers. Warm and heavy, his
hands splayed across her back. It felt completely natural, comfortable and yet strangely exciting. For a
long while he seemed to be apportioning the kiss,
keeping it at a certain level and taking it no deeper.
The moment she realized that he was giving her a last
chance to pull away, he suddenly flipped her onto her
back and rose above her, grinning with delight.

An unexpected gladness shot through her. He
seemed so happy in that moment, and she couldn't
help feeling good about it. What would it hurt to give
in? She wondered. He spoke of love, but it was only
sex, and when he had what he wanted, he would go.
Wouldn't he?

Straddling her hips, he bent his head and gently
nipped at her, catching her bottom lip lightly with his
teeth before melding their mouths again. His tongue
slipped inside, and he spent a long, delicious while
exploring and stroking with leisurely thoroughness
until finally he sprawled full-length atop her, pinning

her to the bed with his weight and plundering her mouth with ruthless efficiency, his hands trapping her head in place. He seemed to be trying to draw her soul from her, and she wrapped her hands around his wrists, but not to discourage him, only to ground herself as desire rapidly swelled.

Finally, he broke the kiss and laid his face in the curve of her neck, his breath hot against her throat, his hands sliding beneath her as he took her into his arms. He simply held her as long as she allowed it, but the poignancy was too great, and she soon felt tears start behind her eyes. Reflexively, she shook off her emotions, and pushed at him with her body until he rose above her once more and sat back on his heels, astride her lower legs.

The certain knowledge of what she wanted shone in his dark eyes, and he reached down to pull her up by her robe, which he then peeled slowly off her shoulders and shoved down her arms until it lay puddled around her hips on the bed. He pulled her gown up to her knees, slipped his hands beneath it and slid them up her thighs, taking the gown with it. Brushing against her quivering belly with his fingertips, he began methodically to cover her face with light, reverent kisses. Then, reaching around her, he yanked the tail of the gown free and drew it up her body and over her head, leaving her naked.

His hungry gaze roved her body as she slowly lowered herself to the mattress again. Tossing aside the gown, he let his hands follow his eyes. When his fingers slipped between her legs, she pulled one from beneath him to give him greater access, rolled her eyes closed and lost herself in the magic. Again and again he stroked and teased with fingers and thumb until desperate need clawed at her, and still he toyed, making her frantic and heedless. Finally, she took matters into her own hands, shoving down his silk pants, wrapping her legs around his hips and pulling him fully atop her with her arms about his neck.

"Yes, yes," he whispered into her ear, "whatever you want, simply take it."

She couldn't think beyond the need to be filled, joined, so she reached down between them and positioned him as she wanted him, then pushed upward, impaling herself. He sank down onto her body with a hiss of pure pleasure, driving her into the mattress as he thrust deeply.

"How I've missed you, missed this."

She squirmed beneath him, needing more even as the pressure inside her made her giddy. "Luc, help me."

"Like this?" he asked, pulling back and driving into her again. She cried out, senses reeling, as he repeated the process. "Is this what you want?"

"Yes!" Had he felt this good before? She wondered, riding a crest of bliss. Could she have forgotten even an instant of such rapture?

He pulled her leg up, holding it high in the crook of his arm as he thrust. "Is this enough?"

"No!" she wailed, thrashing against him. How could it ever be enough?

He lifted her leg even higher and began driving into her like a piston until she spun away from the world and all its fears, until she wept with euphoria, aching with the beauty of it, and lay boneless beneath him. After another moment, he moaned and wrenched free. She felt the hot spurt of his climax on her belly and then the welcome weight of him as he collapsed. Only gradually did she realize that this time they had not used protection—and that only he had stayed sane enough to keep them both free of the surest trap of all.

Alarmed, she lifted a hand to her head just as he groaned, rolled onto his side and gathered her close.

"You astonish me," he murmured against the crown of her head. "How have I lived without that, with you these past days, hmm?"

"You seem to have managed," she pointed out, and heard the echo of another voice, a voice from the past.

You say he needs you, but he's managed just fine until now. I see nothing honorable in you throwing your life away for him!

At the time she'd reasoned that her brother had spoken in anger about her affair with Kenneth, but Wendel had been right, terribly right. Dear heaven, was history repeating itself? What was she doing? Why couldn't she be smart for once?

"Poorly," Luc was saying, "and I'm not ashamed to say so, though perhaps I should be."

The telephone on her bedside table rang, and she reached for it with equal measures of trepidation and relief, half expecting to hear her brother's voice telling her what an eternal disappointment she was to him, half hoping that she would find herself awak-

ening from yet another erotic dream. The voice that
answered her soft greeting was only vaguely familiar.

"Mrs. Lorimer. Sorry to intrude. Lofton here. Lucien isn't answering his phone, and I must speak with
him."

"Hold on."

Frowning, she passed the phone to Luc, who
seemed unsurprised, but then why would he be?
Surely his staff knew exactly where to find him at
any given moment. He put the cordless receiver to
his ear.

"Hello?" He listened a few seconds and sat up,
bracing his back against the headboard. Avis pulled
up the bedcovers and began struggling into her robe.
She hadn't a clue where her gown had ended up.
"Damn. The ambassador himself?" Luc sighed.
"No, it's not convenient, but it is important." He
nodded at something Lofton said and pushed a hand
through his hair. "Very well. Call the pilot, and get
a car out here before you make the other arrangements. Oh, and send me a copy of that speech via
this phone line. Yes, yes, within the hour." He dis-
connected and looked at her apologetically. "I'm
sorry, darling. It's a political situation well outside
Lofton's expertise."

She nodded and tossed back the covers. "I understand." She swivelled, setting her feet to the floor.
"Don't worry. We'll muddle through without you."
Just as she stood, he twisted and caught her by the
wrist.

"I don't want to be away from you. Come with
me. To Prague."

Prague. She shook off a treacherous thrill of excitement. "I have work to do here."

"Pete can handle TexBank for a few days."

She pulled free of him. "I can't leave with you."

"Why not?"

"I-I have friends who would worry about me."

"Call them on the way."

"I can't do that. That's your life. That's how you operate."

"But you're part of my life now," he argued.

"I am not! My life is here. It's always been here! And I need more space than this."

Disappointment darkened those dark eyes. He rolled off the bed and onto his feet, heedless of his nudity. "Space?"

"Yes, space. I'm used to living alone, you know."

"But you don't have to be alone now."

She shook her head. "You just don't get it, do you? I am not turning my life inside out for a temporary thing like…this."

"Temporary?" Anger sparked off him. "That's still how you think of us? Temporary?"

She turned her back on him, uncertain why tears were suddenly gathering in her eyes. "Yes, of course. I've always said so, haven't I?"

"Fine!" he snapped, rustling cloth. He marched around the bed, and she hastily dashed her hands across her eyes. "Then let it be temporary in Prague. Or Tokyo. Seattle. Wherever." Seizing her by the shoulders, he turned her to face him. "Just come with me for now. Better yet, commit the next few weeks to wherever this takes us."

A few weeks of this sweet torture? Longing assailed her, but just that she wanted it so much was reason enough to shake her head. "No."

He cupped her chin in his hand and lifted her face to his, plumbing her eyes with his gaze. She closed them. "You're afraid I'll change your mind," he pronounced softly. She denied it, as she must. "Yes, you are," he refuted gently, "and you should be. Because I will."

He left her standing there shaking her head.

She didn't leave her room until he had gone.

The days flew. Almost before she could catch her breath, he was back, sweeping into her office on the leading edge of a tempest. She fought a thrill at the sight of him and even managed a frown as he pulled her up from her desk chair with one hand on her arm.

"I have something to show you. Come."

It wasn't a request, and she didn't try to pretend that it was, just retrieved her handbag from her desk drawer and allowed him to propel her out of the office and into an elevator.

"What is it?" she finally asked.

He tugged at his cuff links, as impeccably outfitted as ever. "A statement of intention."

"I don't understand."

"You will."

The elevator came to a halt, and the doors slid open. He escorted her across the building lobby and out onto the sidewalk, where a dark-blue limousine waited at the curb. A young man dressed in jeans and a T-shirt stood beside it. He quickly opened the rear door.

"This is Jeff," Lucien said as she ducked into the back seat. "He is our new driver."

"Our?"

He dropped down next to her and closed them inside. "He'll be at the disposal of whoever needs him. For company purposes or personal ones."

"Ah." A Lucien Tyrone project required a Lucien Tyrone driver and limo, of course. It seemed a foolish expense, but she wasn't paying for it.

She heard the driver's door close and glanced at the glass separating them from the front seat. Like the other windows, it was mirrored. They could look out, but no one could see in. She steeled herself, expecting that Luc would kiss her now, but he merely rubbed his hands on his thighs and turned his head to look out the window, saying, "This won't take long."

They rode in tense silence, moving swiftly through the city streets. The driver was obviously highly skilled. Quick and efficient, he seemed fully aware of his route and confident in his handling of the vehicle. She found herself needing to make conversation.

"How was your trip?"

"Busy." Lucien glanced at her then turned back to the window and added in a slightly accusatory tone, "Lonely."

She didn't say anything else. Within moments, the limo slowed and swung off the street onto a lane that traveled between two stately columns of brick topped with pediments in the shape of rearing mustangs.

Avis glanced around her. She hadn't paid attention to anything outside of the limousine and couldn't imagine where they were. It looked like a park. Then the house came into view, a sprawling, single-story of red brick and white tile with a broad porte cochere sheltering the top of the drive and the impressive entry. She slid to the edge of her seat just as the car came to a stop.

"What is this place?"

Lucien opened the door. "I told you, a statement of intention."

He stepped out onto the pavement and reached down for her. She allowed him to help her onto her feet, looking around at the lush gardens and formal facade of a very large house.

"I still don't understand."

"Come inside." He led her along a landscaped walk to the front door, which opened beneath his hand. She saw at once that the house was only partially furnished. They were standing in a small rotunda illuminated by skylight, despite the enormous chandelier of unusual and very modern design sparkling overhead. "This way."

They walked into an immense living room, one wall of which was entirely glass and looked out over a large, beautifully landscaped swimming pool that was fed by a series of waterfalls and fountains constructed of flat rock. "What do you think?" he asked.

She stared at him. "Whose house is this?"

"Mine."

Her eyes flew wide. "*Your* house? Lucien." She shook her head.

"You said you needed space. Well, now you have it, and I have a house in Texas, a *permanent* place of my own."

And a statement of intention. He wasn't giving up on her. If she would not go with him, then he would come to her as often as he could. She didn't know whether to laugh or cry and did a little of each. He grabbed her hand and towed her toward the back of the room and along a short, glass-walled hallway that ended in a single door.

"The bedroom is fully furnished," he said, throwing open that door and pulling her inside. Fully furnished was an understatement. The room was huge, big enough for a small dining table and two chairs, a sofa suite placed before a rock fireplace, bookcases and a built-in armoire, even a desk and computer, not to mention a sumptuous bed facing a full wall of windows overlooking the pool. The front of the house might be brick, but the back of it was all glass.

He released her hand and shrugged out of his suit coat, dropping it to the floor. She knew that look in his eye, and as usual it played havoc with her breathing and started tingles in all the secret recesses of her traitorous body. He loosened his tie.

"Lucien?" It sounded as much a question as a warning even to her own ears.

"I can't wait," he said, dispensing with the tie and beginning to unbutton his shirt. "I want you now."

She backed away, shaking her head. "Don't ask this of me."

"All right," he said, stalking closer. Suddenly he

dipped slightly and swept her off her feet and up into his arms. "I won't ask."

His smile said that he knew perfectly well that she was willing or soon would be, despite everything, despite the cost that she would pay later, that they both would pay later. Perhaps the Greek Tycoon, the billionaire, could afford it, but she could not. Oh, this would break her in so many ways, and at the moment she just couldn't care.

"Do you know what you're doing to me?" she whispered as he carried her to the bed.

"Yes," he answered softly, silkily. "I'm loving you. Get used to it."

Chapter Twelve

Avis sighed and opened her eyes, feeling delightfully refreshed. Naked, she stretched and rolled onto her side, looking at the face of the man sleeping on his stomach beside her, or rather, the half of his face that wasn't smashed into the pillow. Folding the top edge of the covers into a neat cuff beneath her arm, she smiled. This was not the first time she had awakened in his bed over the past several weeks. Being loved by Lucien Tyrone wasn't such a bad thing, after all.

She had her own life, and he had his, jetting in and out regularly. She had come to realize that he returned to San Francisco and his son every third day while on this continent and that it was always his first stop upon returning from overseas. That was as it should be, but she couldn't help feeling sorry for the little boy who so seldom saw his father. Then again, Lucien's family wasn't any of her business, just as her life outside of their moments together wasn't any of his. Not that she had much of a life apart from him and work.

Her friends did call, and she was careful to see them when she could, but only Gwyn knew about Luc, and Avis kept the details to herself, saying only that he'd found himself a place in Fort Worth, that they were both busy and that they were taking it one day at a time. In truth, he was the busy one, though TexBank was shaping up nicely.

Technically they'd decided to call the project Texas Western Heritage Mall and Luxury Apartments, but the shorter TexBank was hard to let go of, so they'd dubbed the project TexWest for short. Avis still thought and said TexBank half the time, though.

Pete was in heaven, wheeling and dealing leases and contracts on a daily basis. Lucien had not really tried to cut him out of the deal, as Avis had feared might happen, so, for the first time in memory, life was as it should be. If moments of unease or dissatisfaction sometimes crept in, well, life was just like that sometimes for everyone. Wasn't it?

"I'm hungry."

Luc's voice yanked her from her reverie. She smiled into his dark eyes. "I'm sure Scott has breakfast waiting."

Scott was the full-time chef Lucien had hired for the Fort Worth house, along with a maid and a part-time groundskeeper. He still manned the kitchen himself on occasion, but his time was short and, as he explained it, he'd rather spend it with her than among the pots and pans, much as he enjoyed cooking.

Lucien lifted onto his side and reached out for her, drawing her in against him. "You first," he said with a wolfish grin, "then breakfast."

She laughed and gladly fed his appetite.

Later, as they were getting dressed, he surprised her by saying that he could stay another night this trip. "We should go out, though," he suggested, "because I've already given Scott the night off, but let's make it someplace private."

She couldn't imagine where that might be around Fort Worth. He had purposely kept a high profile around town, and, as a result, investment opportunities had poured in for him and, to a lesser extent, C&L. An unfortunate consequence, however, was that the man could hardly show his face in public without being recognized and approached.

"Anyplace in mind?" she asked.

He shrugged. "I have a meeting this afternoon, and I expect it to run late, until seven anyway, but I don't want you to have to stay in town until then, so why don't I come to you afterward? Surely you can think of some place in your area where we can eat."

She thought quickly. Maybe it was time for Luc to taste the world in which she lived. Puma Springs didn't have a lot to offer, but Luc was no snob, and while they wouldn't go unnoticed, he wasn't likely to be bothered by anyone, either. "We could try the local steak house. It isn't anything fancy, but the food's good."

He smiled into the mirror as he looped his tie. "It's decided then."

She smiled back. "Better bring a pair of jeans." He paused, prompting her to ask, "You do own a pair of jeans, don't you?"

"I own several pairs. Somewhere."

She laughed, and so did he, both aware that he would have to make time for shopping.

Avis couldn't quite believe her eyes. He not only owned jeans but boots, and wore them very well, with a tight silk T-shirt that left no doubt about the state of his fitness or his masculinity. It was a completely incongruous costume and completely right for Lucien Tyrone. The Greek Tycoon had gone Texas as only the Greek Tycoon could. She refused to take the limo, so Luc sent it back to the city and got behind the wheel of her car. He liked to drive but seldom had the opportunity. Avis was learning that being Luc Tyrone was more complicated and confining that it sometimes seemed.

The steak house had once been a gas station and maintained that theme, though the building had been added onto more than once. The dinner crowd was thin at half-past eight on a weeknight, at least in the dining room. The bar had plenty of patrons, and they kept the single waitress busy enough that she hardly gave Luc a second look. Well, not a third, anyway.

The steaks were fine, but the onion rings really did it for Luc. He admitted that he hadn't eaten the things since college. He'd attended Princeton, followed by Cambridge, much to Hettie Baldwin's delight. He explained this while wolfing down the whole order with his fingers and knocking back a beer, all the while trying to snag the attention of the overworked waitress to request seconds. When that was accomplished, he turned his attention to the rest of the meal, and Avis found that she was having a really good time, watching him observe the locals and tap his toes to the country-and-western music filtering out of the bar, as opposed to being gawked at himself. That ended with the arrival of Heston Witt.

The mayor was putting on weight, and the added puffiness of his face gave his malicious eyes a piggy look as they landed on Avis. He made a beeline for the table. Avis inwardly cringed, but outwardly maintained her composure. Nonetheless Luc, who always seemed attuned to her moods, noticed her reaction.

"What's wrong?"

Before she could answer, Heston was on them. "Out on the town, are we? Don't see much of the heiresses around here lately. Guess we're too low-class for the likes of y'all now."

That would be right, Avis thought, so far as he was concerned, but she said nothing. Luc looked around, sized up the man with a single glance and asked mildly, "And you would be?"

Heston pulled himself up tall. "Heston Witt, the mayor. Don't think I know you."

Luc rose to his feet. "Lucien Tyrone."

Avis thought Witt would swallow his tongue. "Lu-Luc…the Greek Tycoon! Oh, my soul!" He grabbed Luc's hand and began pumping it. "I read you were in Fort Worth, but what are you doing here in our little town?'' His eyes cut to Avis then. ''Well, missy,'' he sneered, ''you've sure come up in the world, thanks to my idiot uncle, climbed right up the ladder over my back.'' He yelped suddenly and yanked his hand free of Luc's. His eyes accused Luc of trying to break that hand, but he did have better sense than to suggest such a thing. Instead he smiled lamely. ''Mr. Tyrone, it's an honor to have you in our fair community regardless…'' He swallowed the rest of that sentence and lightly shook his hand. ''Forgive me for interrupting your dinner.'' He started away, obviously eager to spread the word, then halted uncertainly. ''Please call on me, sir, if I may be of any assistance.'' His gaze darted to Avis. ''I could fill you in on all the pertinent information.'' He leaned in, adding conspiratorially. ''There are matters of which you might not be aware.''

Luc smiled smoothly. ''I am aware, Mr. Mayor, that you are a crude, provincial bore who does not know how to treat a lady in public. That's all I need to know.''

Heston gasped, paled and hurried away as fast as he could waddle. Lucien sat down.

''Charming fellow,'' he said to Avis. ''Would you like me to ruin him?''

''Yes,'' she answered honestly, then, ''No. He's just bitter because his uncle didn't leave him any money to go with the family ranch. He left it to my friends and me instead. Heston's spiteful and petty, but he doesn't really matter, Luc. Just let it go. I have to live in this town, you know, and picking fights with the mayor isn't the most comfortable way to do it.''

He reached across the table to cover her hand with his. "As you wish."

The onion rings came, but not the beer. The frazzled waitress appeared grossly overworked. Luc made a mental note to tip her well and wondered if he ought to speak to her employer. He quickly rejected that idea. This was Avis's turf. She obviously didn't want him throwing his weight around here. Her decision about Heston Witt proved that. She was too softhearted for the Heston Witts of this world.

Little people like Witt were usually beneath Luc's notice. He figured that most of them already had gotten what they deserved out of life, but the way Witt had treated Avis was enough to make him an exception to the rule. Luc hoped he'd broken the fool's hand. Right up until that cretin had imposed himself upon them, the evening had been most enjoyable.

He looked at the onion rings on his plate and rubbed his chin. He really did want that beer. Avis read his thoughts.

"Want me to go get her?"

"No, no, she's already overworked or she wouldn't have forgotten."

Avis pushed back her chair. "I'll go to the bar and get it for you."

He was on his feet in a heartbeat. "You're not to serve me. I'll do it."

"I don't mind."

"I do." He was already moving in that direction, curious about how the locals unwound after a long day. "Want anything?" She shook her head, but he saw that her smile was tight and decided that however interesting the bar might be, they would call it a night as soon as he got that second beer.

The room was dark and loud, but when he approached the bar, two men standing at the end scooted over to make room for him. He caught the bartender's eye.

"Be right with you," the fellow called over the din.

Luc nodded and leaned his elbows on the bar. He heard a voice ask, "Who's that?"

Another man answered. "Some rich dude the Lorimer woman netted."

Luc straightened, but the bartender approached just then. "What can I get you?"

Luc told him, and an instant later had a cold beer in his hand. He paid and stepped away from the bar, but he didn't go back into the dining room just yet, and sure enough, a moment later, the two men began to talk again. Luc moved to stand right behind them.

"The mayor says she's gone from home-wrecker to mistress."

The other one snickered. "The new stud has a lot more going for him than old Ken ever did. Guess she can afford to run in better circles since she inherited Searle's millions."

"Yeah, well, a slut's a slut, I always say."

Cold liquid splashed on Luc's fingers, and he looked down in surprise to find his hand gripped so tightly around the beer bottle that it was in danger of breaking. He was trembling with rage. How dare they speak of Avis that way? He caught the guy by the shoulder and spun him around. The fellow's eyes flew wide in alarm.

"I should take you apart for that filthy remark," Luc snarled.

The man looked down at his shirt front wadded in Lucien's fist. "Hey, get off me!"

People were turning to look. The other man tried to intervene. "He didn't mean nothing, mister. It's just booze talk."

He wanted to bash their heads, but he knew that would only make matters worse for Avis. Besides, the author of that piece of filth was the one who deserved to feel the brunt of his wrath.

Luc shoved the scruffy cowboy away from him and pointed a finger at him. "It's only out of respect for Mrs. Lorimer that I don't break your jaw, but another remark like that will overcome my good manners."

"We didn't mean no harm," the other fellow said, his Adam's apple bobbing, "and it won't happen again." He elbowed his friend. "Will it?" The cowboy reluctantly mumbled a reply.

Luc gave them a hard look, set his beer bottle down on the nearest surface and turned away, scanning the room for Heston Witt. He caught sight of the pudgy mayor bent over a table in the far corner of the room, talking to a couple who sat there. Lucien began to make his way across the room. The crowd parted as he moved through them.

The home-wrecker label confused but did not concern Lucien. The Avis he knew was a woman of integrity, fiercely independent and definitely not his mistress. She was his lover, his love. Perhaps once he'd intended to assign her the role of a true mistress, make her dependent on him, keep her close and at his convenience, but Avis would never accept any relationship that made her less than his equal, which she was in every meaningful sense of the word. Heston Witt's behavior clearly indicated that he had no one but himself to blame for having been cut out of his uncle's will. Lucien wished he'd known the old man now. He'd have liked to have shaken Edwin Searle's hand. Perhaps Edwin would approve of his nervy nephew getting his comeuppance, for life was about to change dramatically for Heston Witt.

Luc stepped up behind Witt just as he turned away from the table where he had been engaged in conversation. The fat mayor bounced off Lucien's chest and looked up with a scowl, which quickly evaporated into something more akin to fear. The music still blared, but conversation seemed to have come to a halt.

"M-M-Mr. Tyrone!"

"Campaigning, Mayor?"

Witt smirked self-importantly. "Oh, I hardly bother with that kind of thing anymore. I've been re-elected repeatedly." The little man drew himself up tall, but not tall enough to keep him from having to bend backward slightly in order to look Luc in the face.

"Is that so?" Lucien smiled benignly. "Well, everything comes to an end, you know."

The mayor chuckled smugly. "I'm very popular around here."

Lucien shed the smile. "A gossip is always popular

in unsavory circles, but not in mine, and my circle is very, very large.''

The mayor gulped. ''I–I don't know what you mean.''

''I mean that I won't stand for you spreading lies and rumors about an innocent woman.''

''Innocent?'' Witt scoffed, then backed up slightly as anger flared in Lucien's eyes. ''A–are you threatening me?''

Lucien brought his mouth close to the mayor's ear. ''Not at all. I'm warning you. You've hurt someone dear to me, spread lies about a woman whom I mean to be a significant and permanent part of my life. I won't tolerate that. This town is no longer going to be comfortable for you, sir. You may want to start thinking about relocating.''

Witt jerked back. ''Don't be absurd! You don't know what she's done to me, what they've all done to me.''

Lucien hauled him close again. ''I know what you've done to yourself, and I advise you to start packing.''

''B–but I was born here! I have deep roots in this community.''

''Not deep enough that I can't dig them out.''

Heston Witt's jowls quivered. ''No one can throw a man out of his own town!''

''My,'' Lucien said, showing his teeth, ''what an uninformed life you lead.''

Witt shivered, his fat jiggling noticeably, and Lucien judged that his message had been received. He released the man, then turned and strode smoothly through the crowd. People looked at him with curiosity. No doubt some had overheard his exchange with the mayor. He didn't really care. Heston Witt was already history; he just didn't know it yet.

Lucien's mind turned to the future, his and Avis's, and he knew, finally, just what that future must be.

He spent the night at her house, and it seemed to Avis that he had taken on a new tenderness and care that frankly unnerved her. She was almost glad when he left her the next morning for Italy. She needed some breathing room suddenly, some time to recoup her energy and strength, to remind herself of who she was and what she really wanted. With that purpose in mind, she set out for Gwyn's coffee shop, hoping for a chat with her old friend. Gwyn had a way of centering Avis's thoughts, sometimes unintentionally.

She was surprised to find Sierra and Sam there, and, when Sierra rose to welcome her with a hug, was shocked to feel a wave of pure envy at the thought of Sierra's pregnancy and Sam's quiet, worshipful pride in it. Shoving that away, she smiled at the friend she had so sorely and shamefully neglected. "You're looking well."

Sierra smoothed her hands down the front of her blouse, pulling it tight and showing off the little mound of her belly. "I feel great. You should see Val, though. She's huge already!"

"Val's a small woman," Sam pointed out, as if reassuring his wife, "and they're further along than we are."

We, Avis thought, as if they were both pregnant.

Why did such a sweet sentiment cause her such a pang?

"Still," Sierra said, "she's huge."

"Maybe it's twins," Avis suggested.

"It's not twins," Gwyn said, arriving with the coffee pot and a hug. "It's a boy, a big boy. Must take after his daddy."

"I didn't know they'd found out!" Sierra exclaimed, clapping her hands together. "Well, that's perfect timing."

"How so?" Avis asked, pulling out a chair at the table.

Sierra dropped back down into her own seat while Gwyn produced a cup and filled it for Avis. "Before you get into that," Gwyn said, looking at Avis, "can I get you anything else? I have sweet rolls, fresh-made this morning."

"No, thanks."

"Thought you'd say that," Gwyn grumped, moving off. "Wait'll you hear what they're cooking up."

"It's not that unusual," Sam protested, sitting down sideways on his chair next to his wife.

"New one on me," Gwyn said over her shoulder.

"Why should the men get left out?" he asked as she went for the sweet roll.

"Left out of what?" Avis wanted to know.

"A baby shower," Sierra answered eagerly. "We want to give one for Val and Ian."

"Val *and* Ian," Avis echoed.

"Well, the guys don't have to take part in all the giggly stuff," Sam said defensively. "We could play cards or barbecue something, but it's not fair to leave us out completely. I mean, these days the men are involved in the pregnancy from the very beginning.''

''I can vouch for that,'' Sierra quipped, then chortled as his cheeks turned red.

''You know what I'm talking about.'' He slid his arms around her, his hand passing possessively over her middle. ''It's my baby, too, and I know that Ian feels the same way about his wife and their pregnancy.''

Sierra turned her head and kissed him on the mouth. Avis had to look away. They seemed at ease with public displays of affection, but she knew that she never could be. She just wasn't meant for that kind of thing, much as she might want to be.

''So what do you think?'' Sierra asked. ''Is it too weird, a couples baby shower?''

Avis looked at Sam's face. Love for Sierra and their child shone in his eyes and excitement over the coming birth literally emanated from his pores. ''No, it's not weird.''

''You'll come then?''

Avis felt her stomach drop. She wasn't part of a couple, not really, not all the time, but she was Val and Ian's friend, as well as Sierra and Sam's. She smiled, refusing even to think of inviting Luc to such an event. This was part of *her* life, not his. ''Of course.''

''Excellent.'' Sierra relaxed into her husband's embrace. ''I'll let you know the particulars as soon as they're decided.''

Avis creamed her coffee and sipped. Not even Lucien's coffee was as good as Gwyn's. She really ought to bring him here. Then again, this place was too personal, too much "hers." She sighed inwardly, wondering why it had to be so complicated.

Sierra groaned. "Not him again."

Avis looked around to see Heston Witt bearing down upon them. The other patrons of the coffee shop, relatively few, thank goodness, stopped what they were doing to watch. Heston came right up to her.

"Call him off," he hissed. He jerked a hand angrily, taking in everyone at the table. "You owe me, damn it, all of you. Just call him off and we'll say it's even!"

Avis could only gape. It was Sam who demanded, "What are you talking about now?"

"That damn tycoon!" Heston muttered. Avis gasped, and he targeted her. "He can't do this to me. You can't let him do this to me. Call him off!"

"I don't know what you're talking about," Avis said softly, painfully aware of eavesdroppers.

"The state attorney general's office called me this morning!" Heston whined. Pulling a handkerchief from his pocket, he mopped his brow. "I haven't done anything. I won't have them poking around in my books, in the city's books. I know he's behind this, and I want it stopped!"

Avis shook her head, confused, appalled. "He wouldn't."

Heston leaned in close. "You have everything. My uncle's money and now a billionaire husband! All I have is my office and this town."

"Husband!" Avis exclaimed. "We're not married."

"As good as," Heston insisted. "He told me so last night."

Avis jerked to her feet. Luc had told Heston that they were getting married? He'd used his influence to have the attorney general investigate the mayor's office? She felt a chill sweep over her, penetrating all the way to the marrow of her bones. She'd thought he understood, thought he'd meant what he said. Beneath the indignation and horror lurked a secret, feminine thrill, but darker emotions overwhelmed and smothered it. Panic crowded close. She couldn't let him take over her life like this.

She had a thing or two to say to Lucien Tyrone. No more Miss Sweetness and Light, going along to get along. He was going to hear her this time or that would be the end for them. Mustering every ounce of her much-prized self-possession, she calmly took her leave.

"Excuse me. I have some personal business to attend to."

She heard Gwyn calling to her. "Avis, think it through."

She nodded, but she knew what she had to do. She had to protect herself. Her hard-won autonomy could not be sacrificed for something as ephemeral as love. Oh, the fairy tale of it might be magically compelling, but she knew the hard truth. Everything in her demanded that she quash this ridiculous notion of a marriage between herself and Lucien Tyrone, everything except one, small, forlorn voice.

Chapter Thirteen

"This is Lucien Tyrone. I am unavailable at the moment. Please leave a message, try again later or call my assistant at—"

Avis hung up the telephone before the impulse to say in a recorded message what should be said in person could win out over her sense of propriety. A mature woman did not issue ultimatums via recordings. She made them face to face, or at least to a live person on the other end of the phone. And, if unsatisfied that her conditions would be met, she walked away with her head held high and simply carried on with her life, the life she chose for herself.

It was that last part that troubled her. Privately, she could admit that her record of walking away from Lucien Tyrone and making it stick hadn't been very impressive thus far, but she was determined to carry through this time. He had to understand that she, and she alone, retained the right to order her own life, and that included dealing with Heston Witt. She had to make him understand for her own sake. With that resolved for the umpteenth time, she decided that she would just wait for him to reappear and set him straight in person.

Then again, what was the point in putting herself through an emotional personal confrontation when the thing could be handled more calmly over the telephone? In fact, now that she thought about it, that seemed the best way, less messy all around. She could have her say then end the conversation before it escalated into undignified shouting and name-calling. Lucien could rant and rave all he wanted in private, and then when they finally met, they'd both be calmer and more rational. It was just a pity that Lucien was not available via his personal cell.

She toyed briefly with the idea of calling up Lofton, but ultimately rejected that notion. Even if he could put her in touch with Lucien, it was bound to be under circumstances less than ideal for her purposes. Besides, it might breach the privacy of her relationship with Lucien in a way she could not foresee. No, it was best to leave Lofton out of the loop entirely.

She tapped a fingernail impatiently against her chin. The sooner she got this over with the better. Already she'd spent two sleepless nights thinking about this, wavering and waffling until she couldn't stand any more. He might still be in San Francisco. She might catch him there. Telling herself that it wasn't cowardice that made her want to do this over the phone rather than face to face, she lifted the receiver and quickly dialed again. She had never called the San Francisco number before, but she had memorized it in case she needed to.

A man answered on the second ring. "Tyrone residence. Who's calling please?"

"Hello, this is Avis Lorimer."

He repeated the name suspiciously. "Avis Lorimer?"

"Yes. Calling for Lucien, ah, Mr. Tyrone."

"I see. From Texas, I presume."

"That's right. May I ask to whom I'm speaking?"

"I'm Archie, Mrs. Tyrone's secretary."

"*Mrs.* Tyrone?" For one insane moment, Avis imagined that it had happened again. Luc had lied to her in the worst possible way. She had gotten involved with a married man. The relationship was at an end. Done. Finished. And good riddance. The next instant, she knew how foolish that notion was. Had she actually hoped, even for an instant, that history actually had repeated itself in that fashion? She shook her head and inadvertently stated aloud what she already knew to be true. "Mrs. Tyrone is Eugenia, Lucien's mother."

"Of course. Could you hold please?"

Confused, Avis didn't manage an answer before the phone clicked and went silent. Several moments later, it clicked again, but the voice that followed was not Lucien's. It was a woman's, deep, husky and heavily flavored but definitely female.

"Hello. Mrs. Lorimer?"

Avis realized that she was speaking to Lucien's mother. "Yes?"

"Your ears must be burning, my dear," Eugenia Tyrone purred. "Isn't that the saying, when someone has been spoken of very recently? We were speaking of you only this morning, my son and I."

Avis felt her throat begin to burn. "I–is Lucien available?"

"No, I am sorry to say, my son is no longer here. He is returning, I believe, to you in Texas. To ask you to marry him." Avis blanched, but Eugenia Tyrone laughed. While pleasant, it didn't sound very merry at all. "Oh, my, I have spoiled the surprise, have I not? Lucien will be very angry with me. But you mustn't let my carelessness influence you. Lucien is quite convinced that he has found the mother his son needs at last."

The mother *his son* needs. Avis put a hand to her throat, feeling as if she were choking.

Eugenia Tyrone went on smoothly, purposefully. "I'm sure you know what great guilt Lucien feels for so often being away from dear Nico, but as I always tell him, it takes a special person to deal with our poor boy. The nurse and therapist are a great help, of course, but—"

"Nurse?" Avis gasped, horrified. "Therapist?"

"Lucien has spoken to you of Nico, his special needs, has he not?"

"Special needs," Avis murmured, her stomach sinking.

"Well, I'm sure you'll manage to cope," Eugenia said hopefully. "Lucien describes you as a kind and gentle woman, soft-spoken, caring. I believe you nursed your late husband through a long illness, did you not? Of course, it isn't the same thing.'' Eugenia sighed. ''I have carried the burden alone for so very long, not that I am complaining. He is my grandson, and I love him, but perhaps I have devoted myself to his care and special needs long enough. Lucien certainly seems to think so, and I'm sure he knows best. Don't you agree?''

Avis could only babble. ''I, ah, I–I'm sure Lucien has his son's best interest at heart. P-please excuse me, Mrs. Tyrone, I'm afraid I have to go. If you speak to Lucien before…ah, no, never mind. Goodbye, Mrs. Tyrone.'' Avis dropped the telephone receiver into the cradle as if it were a hot rock.

She doubled over, a muscle in her abdomen cramping with sudden ferocity. She could barely breathe. He wasn't married, oh no, but this *was* history repeating itself! She tried to think of all the times Lucien had mentioned Nicholas and realized that they had been relatively few and spectacularly uninformative. Now she understood why. The boy had some terrible malady that required constant attention and care—and Lucien had pegged her for the job!

No wonder he was suddenly talking marriage. His son needed a mother, a caretaker, apparently, a nurse, and who better than a childless widow once devoted to the care of an ailing spouse? If Lucien also got a willing bed partner into the bargain, what more could he ask for? No doubt she was meant to be grateful that he would punish Heston Witt for her, or was it more about silencing Heston, quelling any unsavory rumors about the future Mrs. Lucien Tyrone? It all made horrible sense now.

She got up from the side of her bed and paced a few steps away, refusing to think of that little boy in San Francisco. He wasn't her responsibility, and she wouldn't let Lucien make him her responsibility. She closed her eyes and wondered why she was surprised, disappointed, hurt, when she'd known all along how it would be. She lifted her shoulders and felt resolution settle there as the last doubts about her course of action fell away. She felt a certain amount of grief, but relief was there, also, and she held on to that. Desperately.

Lucien checked the table once more. A cloth of gold brocade draped the round top. Two china plates on expensive crystal chargers rested at a slight angle to each other, flanked by identical rows of heavy, gold-inlaid flatware. Red napkins intricately folded into the shape of roses lay dead center on the plates, which were crowned with an array of crystal flutes. A red vase of white roses and trailing ivy formed the centerpiece. Behind it stood a silver-and-gold wine bucket chilling an especially expensive vintage of champagne. A blue velvet jeweler's tray containing a fortune in diamond rings sat open to one side.

Too obvious, he decided, and snapped the rectangular box closed, then on second thought stashed it conveniently to hand on the second tier of the serving tray, where the opening courses of dinner waited. He'd sent a single rose and a handwritten note to her office this morning, then come straight here from the airport to make the arrangements.

He'd tried to keep the menu simple: brie encroute, green salad, medallions of beef, chilled asparagus, miniature potatoes and mushrooms with rosemary, brioche, and raspberry sherbet in chocolate cups for dessert. He'd warned Scott that they might not get to dessert.

Belatedly he realized that he'd again wiped his sweaty palms on the legs of his pleated, olive-green trousers. At this rate they'd have no crease left at all by the time she arrived. He glanced wistfully at the fireplace. Texas was damnably hot, making a romantic fire out of the question. The many candles flickering around the darkened room would have to do. His gaze moved to the bed with its covers folded back neatly, and his pulse jumped. To distract himself, he checked the fold of the cuffs of his sleeves, rolled back to reveal his tanned forearms. Likewise, the collar and top few buttons of the soft, loose, white lawn shirt were left open.

He'd felt poised on a knife edge all day, his nerves tingling, heart racing. This was a step he had never really expected to take, and he knew that it would come as a shock to Avis, but surely over these past weeks she had come to realize what he had. They were good together. They belonged together. He would protect her, cosset her as no one ever had. He would indulge her shamefully, please her in every possible way, and take his own pleasure in doing so.

He imagined that she would want to work with him, become a significant and integral part of his operations. He saw them as a team, moving around the world, managing their businesses, homes and growing family together, but always taking time for each other and those they loved. Perhaps he would build her a great house in Puma Springs, where Nico would thrive in the Texas sun and other children would be born. He laughed, imagining brothers and sisters for Nico, but then he thought of his mother in a little nothing town in Texas, and he frowned.

As he had expected, Eugenia was not best pleased about his plans to remarry. Had she been able to choose a traditional, obedient Greek wife for him, someone she could easily bully and manipulate, she would have been somewhat mollified, but that was a battle Lucien had already fought and won and had no intention of repeating. Still, he didn't fool himself that Avis Lorimer would not continue to complicate his life. She couldn't know how much. It was one of the reasons why he hadn't already remarried, but his conviction that he had found his mate overrode all other concerns.

He heard the car and checked his watch, heart quickening. About time. Past time, really, but that was Avis, always quietly, stubbornly calling the tune. She didn't scream and throw everything that came to hand the way his mother did, thank God, and neither did she manipulate and scheme, but he thought she was sometimes even more difficult to deal with than Eugenia—and more worth the bother. He smiled and hurried through the house, more eager to see her with every step, but when he opened the door, he found only Jeff standing there, cap in his hand.

A cold fist seized Lucien's heart.

"What is it? Where is Mrs. Lorimer?"

The young driver coughed behind his hand and scuffed his feet on the paving stone. "She, uh, she said to tell you, 'No, thanks.'"

"No, thanks?" he echoed, suddenly aware of a pain in the top of his head, as if his blood pressure had just shot through it. "To dinner?"

Jeff shrugged sheepishly. "I guess. Then she said I was never to come for her again."

"Never to come—" Lucien broke off, momentarily blinded by the sudden anger. The stubborn little fool. Surely she wasn't trying to break it off with him again. He reached for a reasonable tone. "Are you saying that she objected to traveling by limousine?"

Jeff cleared his throat. "I don't think so." He grimaced and blurted, "She said to tell you that she never wants to see you again, either."

Lucien felt the words like hammer blows. They rained down on him from nowhere, as unexpected as demons popping up on his shoulders. It made no sense whatsoever. He tried to think. Surely she wasn't exercised over Heston Witt. He hadn't wanted to say anything about the incident in the bar, hadn't wanted to hurt and embarrass her with the gossip being spread, but perhaps he should have made it clear that he meant to remove the man from their lives. Perhaps he should have made a lot of things clear, but then he thought he had. In fact, he was quite sure that the woman knew exactly how he felt about her. She had to, and now she thought she could just call a halt, send him on his way?

"We'll see about that," he growled, swinging out of the door and around the driver in one smooth movement. He jerked a hand angrily at the car as he strode toward it. "Go! Find her. Start where you left her. And be quick about it!"

He yanked open the door and dropped down into the seat, slamming himself inside. Jeff was just a heartbeat behind him, and in quick order they were speeding down the drive, the limo gliding over the pavement. His mind worked furiously, recalling actions and reactions. He remembered especially the words she'd shouted at him the night he'd followed her home.

I'm not twenty years old anymore…not a thing you can own! I'm not just some pretty convenience you can pick up on a whim… I have my own life… thoughts…goals! I won't let you put me back into a box of obligation and…

He put a hand to his forehead, thinking how hard he'd worked to show her that her feelings and fears mattered to him, would always matter to him. Anger, disappointment, worry all combined into a volatile mix that churned in his gut until he felt ill by the time the limo screeched to a halt in front of her office building. He slammed out of the car and sprinted inside, opting for the stairs, too impatient for the elevator.

He broke out onto her floor, swept down the hall and pushed through the door to her office. Pete stood at the counter making a note. He looked up and smiled.

"Hello, Luc."

"Where is she?" Lucien demanded.

It didn't take a genius to figure out whom Lucien meant. "I think she's still in her office."

He started forward as if to get the door for Lucien, but in three strides Luc had left him behind. Thrusting open the door himself, he stalked inside.

Avis stood at the bank of windows that overlooked Sundance Square, her arms wrapped tightly about her middle. She didn't turn when her door opened, didn't lift her head or shift in any way, but she knew who was there and why.

"I don't want to see you, Lucien. Please go away."

The softness of her tone, the gentle way she spoke told him everything. She meant it. For some insane reason the woman actually meant it. And yet, she didn't mean it at all. This was the paradox that was Avis Lorimer. He closed the door practically in Pete's face.

"Liar," he said harshly, and she spun, indignation spurring her.

"I'm not the liar!"

"You are implying that I am?"

She turned aside. "I called San Francisco."

Mild shock jolted him. "And?"

"I spoke to Mrs. Tyrone."

He frowned at that. "Mrs. Tyrone? The *only* Mrs. Tyrone at the moment is my mother." Avis just looked at him. "You didn't think…? Even for an instant…"

She smiled tightly, then shook her head. "I

couldn't be caught like that again. I'd have known this time.''

''This time?'' he asked, and watched her take a deep breath.

''My husband, Kenneth, was married when we became involved. I didn't know it,'' she added quickly, ''not until it was too late.''

He frowned, remembering what he'd heard in the bar. *From home-wrecker to mistress…* He hadn't believed it then. He still didn't. ''Explain that. How was it too late?''

She shook her head, but then she said, ''When the scandal broke, he lost everything: his position at the university, marriage, family, home, everything.''

Lucien digested that quickly. ''And you thought it was your fault? He lied to you, and you thought it was your fault?''

''I allowed it to happen,'' she admitted softly, ''just as I've allowed what's happened between you and me.''

Lucien rocked back on his heels. ''It's not the same thing. That was a different time and place and situation.''

She pinned him with angry eyes. ''Don't say I was too young to know what I was doing! I did know. I made a choice. The wrong one, and I lived with it, but not this time. I'm sorry, but not this time!''

He gaped at her. ''Think what you are saying.''

''I know exactly what I'm saying,'' she snapped. ''I let myself be trapped once, but not again. Never again.''

''Trapped! How were you trapped?''

"I was all he had!" she cried. "Then he became ill. How could I leave? I couldn't leave!"

"I am not Kenneth Lorimer!" he shouted, understanding all too clearly now. "How could you believe that I would trap you? How could I possibly?" He spread his arms, at a loss. "I love you, Avis."

She put her hands over her ears and shook her head. "What difference does that make? You think you love me because I fit, that's all."

He walked across the room, rubbing his aching temples. "You say it like it's nothing." He dropped his hands. "Yes, you fit. We fit. Like hand and glove, we fit. Like we were made for each other."

"Oh, yes, how perfect. Let's see, first requirement, a compliant bed partner."

He almost laughed. "I'm Lucien Tyrone. Not to sound arrogant, but I can find *compliant* bed partners by the thousand, in every country, all over the world, but I'm smart enough to know that it has less to do with me than with my bank account. I want much more than *compliance,* believe me."

She glared at him resentfully, but went on. "Second requirement. Soft-spoken, gentle."

"I've had my share of shrews," he said unapologetically.

She ignored that, folding her arms. "A good mother?"

That was unexpected, but reasonable. "I expect so, yes."

"With an understanding of the business world and its demands, particularly on you."

"Obviously."

She faced him squarely and said, very pointedly, "An experienced nurse."

That did not compute. "A *nurse?*" He screwed up his face to show his confusion. "Do I look like I need a nurse? Let me assure you, I am perfectly healthy and expect to stay that way. But perhaps you want a doctor's note? A physical examination? Absurd as that is, I'm willing to oblige you."

"And what of your son?" she asked mildly.

He didn't know what to say at first. Then he realized that she knew about Nicholas. It all clicked into place, and he understood exactly whom he had to thank for it. He would wring her neck, the meddling old banshee. He knew, too, that nothing he could say now would convince Avis that he had not courted her as a nursemaid for his poor dear boy. He was stymied. He should have told her already, explained the situation, but his son's problems were a very tender spot for him, a constant ache. And he'd been afraid of her reaction.

"It's not what you think."

"Isn't it?"

For a moment he could only stare at her as the enormity of this latest revelation settled over him. Could she really believe that she could only be wanted for what she could supply to others? Yes, apparently she could.

"Has no one else ever loved you?" he heard himself ask, but then he shook his head and began talking his way through it. "Kenneth must have loved you. What man wouldn't?" She turned away, but he went on, trying to make her understand what he himself was only beginning to. "But selfishly, only for what you could bring to him. He didn't care what it cost you or what you felt for him, and obviously he didn't deserve you. He was all wrong for you, in fact, but the selfish bastard helped himself anyway, because he knew what a jewel he'd found. He trapped you. No doubt you're right about that. He used your goodness and your sweetness to tie you to him. How else could he hope to hold you? Because you sure as hell didn't love him."

She bowed her head at that, and he stepped closer, pulling her into his arms. She resisted at first, but not very hard and not very long. He smiled when she melted against him. She used acquiescence like a weapon, pretending to give in when she never really yielded at all, but that was not what was happening here, what had been happening since he'd come to Texas. She didn't seem to know it yet, but she wanted, needed to yield to him, to be loved by him. It was innate in her, as natural as her soft femininity and lush beauty, and yet beneath her feminine softness she was all steel, this woman, as strong as anyone he'd ever known. But what standards she held herself to! Inhuman standards. Unfair standards.

He tilted her face up to his. "I told you that I would learn all your secrets. I should have told you all of mine. Now I'll have to show you."

She frowned. "Show me what?"

He sighed, thinking of the lovely dinner that they would never eat, the ring she would not now choose, the completely decadent, deeply erotic manner in which he had intended to celebrate, but then he shook his head. It was her tune. He would play it as she demanded.

"We're going to San Francisco. It's time you met Nico and my mother."

She shoved out of his embrace. "No, I'm not."

"Yes, you are," he insisted flatly. "It's the only way to show you what being a permanent part of my life would really mean."

She shook her head desperately. "I *can't* go with you. I won't."

"You can, and you will. I mean it, Avis. If I have to bind you hand and foot and carry you out of here over my shoulder, you're getting on that plane with me."

"You wouldn't dare."

He would, but he didn't say so, not while he still held a trump card. "I'll pull the plug on TexWest."

"Now?" she scoffed. "And lose millions? I don't think so. You're too good a businessman, Lucien."

"This is more important than business," he told her honestly. "*You* are more important than business, Avis. *We* are more important." She blinked, almost persuaded. "And I have the millions to lose," he added ruthlessly. "Do you? Does Pete?"

She glared at him, and her chin began to tremble. "That's not fair."

"No, it isn't, but you force my hand."

"It won't change anything!" she insisted.

"Then why not go?" he countered. He didn't have to point out how much she had to lose by refusing to do so.

She all but stamped her foot, and it both amused

and grieved him to watch her struggle with her own sense of decorum. Dear heaven, if she could only understand how much he loved her!

"I'll have to go home and pack a bag," she grumbled.

"Not necessary. We won't be gone that long, a night or two at most. We'll pick up what little you need on the way." He snagged her hand. "Come. The sooner we leave, the sooner you'll see."

"The sooner *you'll* see," she vowed, yanking free of him, "because I'm not going to change my mind, and you can't make me."

"No," he agreed softly, "I can't make you."

"And I *will* pack a bag before we leave," she insisted.

He sighed. They were going to argue again. Well, what was one more spat when he was already engaged in the fight of his life? It was the truth, but he knew without the slightest shred of doubt that if in the end he prevailed, it would be because she had finally, once and for all, yielded her stubborn, wounded heart.

He could not settle for anything less.

Chapter Fourteen

Avis could not believe what she was seeing. Terrace upon terrace spilled color onto the slope of the hillside. Flowers of every hue and variety ran riot alongside the lane, occasionally crossing it via enormous trellises placed at irregular intervals. The air here was truly "softer" than that in Texas, just as Lucien had described it, because moisture overlaid everything, as if the spray from a powerful waterfall had permeated not only the air but the light, as well as all substance. Even her skin had taken on a dewy feeling. Fortunately, the mildness of the temperature kept the effects of the humidity from overwhelming her lungs, but the scenery was almost too much to take in. In fact, ever since the limo had turned through the manned gate at the foot of the hill, she'd had a difficult time keeping her mouth closed as every bend in the curving road revealed an even more stunning vista. It was like living in a rainbow.

She looked at the man next to her. They had spoken little since they'd boarded his private jet, and she couldn't help feeling that he was indulging himself in a protracted sulk. Perhaps she had been particularly dogged in convincing him that she did, indeed, have to pack a bag before she could accompany him to California, but he had coerced her into the trip, and it was only reasonable, after all. What difference did a couple of hours make? And how was she to know that a sudden thunderstorm in New Mexico would delay their flight program even further? Besides, arriving in the early morning seemed infinitely preferable to the dead of night to her, even if she had caught little sleep on the airplane.

Lucien had seemed to rest well enough. He should have, given that he'd slept in a real bed in the rear compartment of the jet, a comfort in which she had repeatedly declined to join him. It was no wonder then that, after availing himself of an electric razor kept on the luxuriously outfitted jet, he looked fresh as a daisy, if a little out of character in his loose clothing. She, on the other hand, wanted a hot bath and the judicious application of a can of hair spray. She could literally feel her hair curling, probably in an outlandishly untidy fashion, but as she kept reminding herself, she wasn't here to impress anyone. She was doing what she had to do to protect her business and make her point, that any further association between them was impossible and unwanted. It just seemed grossly unfair that this place should be as appealing as its owner.

She kept quiet as long as she could, but when the house itself finally came into view, a sprawling two-story palace of white rock and golden marble, she found words tumbling out of her mouth unimpeded. "I can't believe this isn't enough for you."

He arched both brows. "What is enough, Avis? Should I stay here in this lovely place and grow orchids, perhaps? You are a simple woman in many ways, you have made a home and a life for yourself, you live comfortably on the income from your investments, but do you sit in your sweet little house and read magazines all day? No. You are actively seeking to accomplish more, to *be* more. So you tell me, what is enough, Avis? What is it that drives you?"

The comparison seemed uneven to her. "You have so much more than me, though."

"Do I?" He shook his head. "We both have all we need materially. We both have careers. I'd even say we have an acute business sense in common. Power can be a great burden, frankly, and at any rate it seems to matter little to you, except on a personal level, and you already have the right and the means to make your own choices and decisions, so I'd say we're equals there. We each have friends, places where we belong." He shrugged. "Perhaps the only thing I have that you do not is family, and that I would gladly give you."

Troubled, she turned her gaze out the window, only

to hear herself saying, "I have an older brother." She felt Lucien's surprise.

"I don't believe you've spoken of him before."

She clamped her jaws, but the words slid free anyway. "He cut all ties with me when I chose to stand by Kenneth." Feeling a sudden chill, she rubbed her hands over her forearms.

"Ah," Lucien said. "A coward, then."

Her head turned sharply. "How can you say that? You don't even know him."

"I know what kind of people cut themselves off from love. It takes strength and courage to love and support someone even when they make mistakes, and since everyone makes mistakes, it follows that all love requires courage. Those who cannot face the risk of disappointment and heartache cut themselves off. They live in a dull, safe world of black and white, devoid of risk *and* reward, pain *and* joy. I am sorry for him."

Avis had always believed that she had disappointed Wendel so thoroughly that he'd had no choice but to cut her out of his life. She knew from periodically reaching out to him over the years that he had never married. He still lived alone in the house where they had lived as children. Had she thought him wise for that? Was she a coward, as well? She felt shaken, but she told herself that she was too tired to make sense of anything just now.

The long vehicle glided to a stop beneath a broad portico paved with creamy, closely fitted stone, but the driver did not get out. Instead, a small, fastidious man in a narrow black suit, white shirt and black tie hurried down the broad, elaborately landscaped and covered walk to the car.

"Archie," Lucien announced tersely, "Mother's lapdog."

The door at his elbow swung open just then, and he climbed up out of the car, reaching down again for her. She allowed him to help her out of the car and to her feet, then she stepped away from him and smiled shyly at the little man peering curiously at her. He stood with pale, bony hands clasped at chest height, and she saw that his narrow head was not bald as she'd first thought. Instead, his thinning light brown hair had been ruthlessly combed, oiled and plastered to his scalp. Tempted to try to smooth her own hair, she fought to keep her hands at her sides.

"Archibald," Lucien said by way of greeting.

The little man's elongated nostrils flared as if he'd caught an unpleasant scent, and he lifted his chin defensively before turning his attention once more to Avis. "Mrs. Lorimer," he gushed, taking one of her hands in both of his soft, limp ones. "I am Archie. I believe we spoke yesterday on the telephone."

"Yes, I remember."

He inclined his head with obvious satisfaction and gave her back her hand. "Mrs. Tyrone has prepared a small repast in your honor. Won't you follow me?" He executed a smart pirouette and started back up the walk.

"I assure you," Lucien told her dryly, falling in beside her as she followed along, "Mother has prepared nothing in your honor. She's merely ordered coffee in the sunroom, which she feels shows her to best advantage at this time of morning.''

Uncertain that anyone could be so scheming or vain, Avis sent him a doubtful look, and for some reason the troublesome man put his head back and laughed.

''Is it any wonder that I love you?'' he asked. He drew her to a halt then, and held her by the upper arms with his hands, looking intently into her eyes. ''You mustn't let her get to you. My mother does not command my life. She tries, and in all honesty, for Nico's sake she's been almost indispensable, but I learned very young to stand up to her.'' He smiled in a lopsided fashion. ''Come to think of it, that may have been her greatest gift to me. Just remember, I am on your side.''

''My side?'' she scoffed. ''It isn't a war, you know.''

''With Mother,'' he said, ''it is always war.''

''She seemed friendly enough on the telephone.''

''She is very friendly, even charming, when it suits her, but do not think, my love, that you will be welcomed.'' She frowned. ''Except by me,'' he added, clapping a hand to the nape of her neck. He kissed her quickly on the mouth. ''Come,'' he said, wrapping his arm around her, ''to battle.''

Eugenia Tyrone sat in a delicate wingback chair upholstered in ivory damask. Behind her, a wall of windows provided a backdrop reminiscent of a Monet landscape, while around her the spring-green walls of an enormous room trimmed in ivory opulence and lavishly furnished to the point of gold-leafed tables, framed her like a living painting. Garbed in deep red, she sat erect on the edge of the seat cushion, ankles crossed, tiny, manicured hands folded in her lap. Apart from her eyes, which were very large and very black, her facial features were petite, almost elfin, and this was accentuated by her slate-gray hair, cropped at chin-length and worn full and wispy. At a distance, she looked much too young to be Lucien's mother. Up close, she wore her age well, displaying the confidence of a beautiful woman who knew that she outshone all her contemporaries in every way.

She smiled in a practiced manner and indicated a chair near hers for Avis before lifting an Elizabeth Taylor eyebrow at her son. Lucien obediently moved forward and placed a kiss on her cheek.

"Mother. Allow me to present Mrs. Avis Lorimer. Avis, my mother, Eugenia."

From her seat, Avis inclined her head. "A pleasure to meet you, ma'am."

Eugenia inclined her head, a queen accepting her due. "Will you take coffee?"

"Yes, thank you."

Eugenia waved a hand toward a serving cart standing just out of her own reach. "Luc, be a dear. I'm sure you know how your little friend likes her coffee." She curved her mouth at Avis. "I find it so awkward to have servants about at times like these, do you not agree?"

"Times like these, Mother?" Lucien interrupted, pouring coffee into a delicate china cup. "And what sort of time would this be, hmm? The first bloodletting, perhaps?''

Eugenia did not so much as indicate that she had heard him. She focused entirely on Avis. ''You are quite lovely, Mrs. Lorimer, even as rumpled as you are from your journey.''

Avis blanched, painfully aware of her wrinkled slacks, simple tunic and frizzing hair.

''Ignore her, darling,'' Lucien said calmly, bringing her the cup and saucer.

She ignored him instead, beyond taking the cup onto her knee, and he returned to the serving cart. ''Thank you, ma'am, and please call me Avis.''

''You are not quite what I expected, Avis,'' Eugenia said bluntly. ''Lucien's late wife was tall and slender, a fashion model in Europe, a natural, classic beauty.''

''Except, of course, for the breast implants that she got after Mother harped about her 'boyish' figure,'' Lucien added, piling fruit and pastries onto a plate. Avis struggled to contain her shock.

''Perhaps she was too slender at first,'' Eugenia commented, her gaze sliding away.

''Perhaps she was,'' Lucien conceded, turning a meaningful look over his shoulder at Avis, ''but I prefer a natural figure. And strength of character.''

Avis looked down at the coffee she had yet to taste. It was the perfect shade of brown. She lifted the cup to her mouth and sipped. The brew was strong and scalding but without any trace of bitterness. Lucien appeared with an encouraging smile and a plate of food, which he placed on the table before her, and a napkin, which he draped over her lap.

"Avis is not Althea, Mother," he said approvingly. "She won't flee the room in tears at your poorly veiled barbs."

"How sad for you," Eugenia said snidely. "You will have to forego the pleasure of comforting her in bed."

Lucien laughed. "I assure you, Mother, I forego no pleasures in her bed."

Avis felt her face flame. She briefly considered leaving the room, not in a bolt but sedately and with dignity. She would not, however, give Eugenia Tyrone the satisfaction. She took another sip of coffee and reached for a piece of melon.

"I see no ring on her finger," Eugenia said to Lucien. "Perhaps your selection of diamonds was not equal to her tastes."

Avis looked up sharply at that, but Lucien merely replied, "She hasn't had the opportunity to choose, as I have not yet proposed." He looked at Avis and added, "I had intended to, but I realized that it wouldn't be fair until you'd had a chance to understand what you'd be getting into."

Something inside Avis melted at that, and she quickly looked at her plate, reminding herself why she had come here.

"Let us be frank, my dear," Eugenia said imperiously. "Lucien needs a wife accustomed to his world, an equal in every way."

"Not a nurse for his son?" Avis inquired mildly,

wincing inwardly as the words slipped out. Eugenia had the grace to color.

"*I* care for Nicholas," she asserted flatly. "He won't accept you."

"Perhaps he won't," Lucien snapped, "and perhaps one day he will. Surely even you hope for that, Mother."

"Of course, I do!" Eugenia cried, temper flashing in her dark eyes. "How dare you question my love for that boy!"

"I do no such thing," Lucien replied calmly, "but how much is your concern for Nico and how much is your need to maintain control of the family?"

Eugenia hit her feet in a torrent of Greek. Lucien replied calmly in kind, then contrived to look bored, filling a cup and plate for himself as she shrieked. Avis openly gaped. No wonder he wanted a polite, calm woman! His share of shrews, indeed. Presently Eugenia wore out her temper and turned her attention once again to Avis, chin high as she struggled for composure.

"I have nothing against you personally."

"That's true," Lucien put in wryly. "She would behave in as beastly a manner to any woman whom she did not handpick for me."

"As if *that* could happen!" Eugenia objected.

"True again," Lucien said unrepentantly.

Eugenia threw up her hands in obvious exasperation and said to Avis, "His father spoiled him. I have never been able to make him see reason."

"Difficult," Lucien muttered, "when you have never been able to see reason yourself."

"So I have to tell *you*," Eugenia went on dog-gedly, "that I cannot welcome this intrusion. My grandson does not need you in his life. He has enough to deal with. I cannot fathom why Lucien would in-flict anything else on him. Should you choose to join this family, I have to warn you that it will not be easy." With that she marched from the room, her small feet clapping smartly against the Persian rugs covering the marble floors.

Lucien struck a relaxed pose by the serving cart. "I think that went very well."

Avis plunked down her cup and saucer next to her food plate. "You did try to warn me."

"Ah, but as my father used to say, Eugenia defies description. She must be experienced." He picked up his own cup and carried it to the seat Eugenia had vacated. "The thing about Mother is, you must never rise to the bait or take her emotional outbursts too personally."

"She *is* very emotional," Avis conceded in a care-ful tone.

"Mother is pure emotion," Lucien said, "and it's of her nature to fight for supremacy."

"Well, at least I know where you got it," Avis quipped.

He chuckled. "You didn't know my father. He was her equal in every way, and believe it or not, it was a very happy marriage. He loved her insanely, and much to her disgust, it was mutual."

Avis was having a little trouble picturing that. "They got along then?"

"Rarely. But they each took great pride in the

other's strength. She has always referred to him as her 'lion,' and even when he seemed angry enough to throttle her, that deep pride was always there in his eyes. He told me once that a woman who will not fight you is not worth fighting for.'' He smiled with remembrance and added, ''I understand that better since I met you.''

Avis lifted both eyebrows. ''Lucien, I am nothing like that. I hate confrontation.''

''But you will stand resolute, nonetheless. You'll smile and lower your eyes and refuse to budge an inch until you're utterly convinced, until every argument has been overcome. It's absolutely maddening. And unspeakably precious. Strength comes in many forms, my love, and I prefer yours to all others I have seen. Now eat your breakfast. I'm sure we have another unpleasant scene ahead of us.''

Avis fought through a sense of warm pleasure to concentrate on what was most important. Nicholas. She took a deep breath, blew it out again through her nostrils and helped herself to a strawberry. Obviously, she needed fortification. Even Lucien seemed to. She noticed as he drank deeply of his coffee that his brow seemed tight, a tiny furrow appearing between his eyes. Perhaps he had not rested as well as she'd thought. Perhaps much was not as she'd thought. Deflated, she ate her breakfast in silence, wondering just how much danger her resolve was in.

Nicholas Tyrone occupied an entire wing of the Tyrone mansion, if such a mundane term could describe the palatial house. There were rooms for everything: clothes, toys, media, private dining and visiting, instruction, nurses, nannies, therapy. Avis didn't ask what sort of therapy the boy required, realizing that she would know soon enough. Presently Lucien opened the door to a small library, and a plump, thirtyish woman in flowered scrubs came immediately to her feet. Beside her a small boy with thick, curly blond hair bent his head over a picture book.

"Oh, Mr. Lucien," she said, delight and welcome in her voice. "We didn't expect you back so soon." She bent toward the boy, tucking her hands between her knees. "Nicholas, your father is here." The child did not respond. She straightened, her smile still in place. "He loves this book, so it's now part of our reward system. If I'd known you were coming, I wouldn't have given it to him, but he's worked very hard this morning."

"Hard work deserves reward," Lucien said heartily, but he lifted a hand to Avis, silently asking her to stay in place, before he approached his son. Nearing the table, he went down on his haunches, bringing his face level with the boy's. "Hello, son." The boy began to rock slightly, but he looked up briefly and smiled at his father.

"My b–book," he said, focusing once more on the picture. Avis craned her neck a little to see what was so interesting and found that what engrossed him so was a simple photo of a boy bending to pick up a ball from the ground.

"What are you looking at here?" Lucien asked with interest.

The boy began pointing to various aspects of the picture. "Boy. Shoes. Shirt. S-socks. Ties. P-pants. Ball. S-sidewalk. Tree. Grass. D-dirt. S-sky. Light."

"Very good," Lucien praised. "And what is the picture about?"

"The boy is going to p–play with the ball."

"That sounds like fun."

"Yeah." He shook his head. "Don't throw it."

"You prefer to roll the ball, don't you?"

"Don't throw it," Nicholas said firmly and went back to studying the picture.

Lucien waited a moment then said, "I've brought someone to meet you." He motioned to Avis, and she started forward, but suddenly Nicholas jerked around stiffly and looked at her. His gaze seemed to bounce off her and fly around the room. He shoved his chair back and rose, one hand drawn up tightly against his chest.

"No!" he yelled. "Book! I want my book!"

The nurse backed away, keeping her hands to herself and looking at Lucien apologetically. Lucien nodded, rose and seized the boy by both arms, holding him still but keeping their faces level. "You can look at your book in a moment," he said calmly. "She's not here for you. She's my friend. I only want you to meet her. All right? We're learning how to be polite, remember?"

The boy calmed, but his gaze stayed on the book on the table. Lucien rose to his full height and turned to face Avis, one hand sliding across the boy's shoulders comfortingly. He beckoned her closer. "Avis, this is my son, Nico."

She walked forward uncertainly, attempting to make eye contact. "Hello."

The boy stared at the book. "Say hello to Avis, Nicholas," Lucien instructed. The boy ignored him. Lucien tightened his embrace slightly and firmed his voice. "Be a polite boy and say hello."

The child squirmed, trying to shrug off his father's arm, and Avis's heart went out to him. "Don't push, Lucien," she pleaded softly, but he shot her a sharp glance and repeated himself.

"Say hello to Avis."

Finally the boy's gaze, dark as night, slid over her. "Hello," he said quite cordially.

Lucien hugged him. "Thank you. Now you may go back to your book while I have a word with Nurse."

The boy eagerly returned to his chair and bent low over the photo once more, seemingly oblivious to all else. Lucien led the nurse over to Avis and then led the pair of them to the door. "Karen, this is Mrs. Lorimer." The nurse offered her hand and a warm smile, both of which Avis accepted. "Karen is specially trained in treating autistic children," Lucien told Avis smoothly. Then he turned his attention to the nurse once more. "Everything going well?"

"Oh, yes. He's making real strides. As I told you last time, he has his alphabet and corresponding sounds down well now, and we're moving slowly into an actual reading program."

"Any concerns?"

"Just the one we've already spoken about. He should have gone to group therapy today."

Lucien sighed. "I'll speak to Mother again."

"She doesn't like him to go immediately after you've visited," the nurse said, "but I don't see any stress-related behaviors in relation to that, and the older he gets the more he needs socialization therapy."

Lucien nodded. "I understand. Thank you, Karen. I'll be back later this afternoon."

"He'll like that," the nurse said, turning away. As Lucien escorted her from the room, Avis heard the nurse say to Nicholas, "I'm going to reset the timer now. You can look at your book until the bell rings."

Lucien pulled the door closed. "Well," he said, "now you know."

Avis bit her lip, conflicted but sympathetic. "Lucien, I'm so sorry."

He shook his head. "They've made great strides in treatment, and happily he has a good chance at a fairly normal life. I, on the other hand, have little hope for normal parenthood, at least so far as Nico is concerned. His environment must be carefully controlled. Every change must be integrated slowly and purposefully, or the stimuli simply overwhelms him. Eventually, he'll learn to cope well enough to interact comfortably. We're fortunate that he's very, very bright. He's also a little spoiled, I'm afraid."

"And would be with or without the autism, I suspect," she offered lightly.

He smiled in agreement. "The point is, he doesn't need what we might think of as a normal father or a normal mother, come to that. And frankly, a step-mother at this point is a real complication, though if I didn't believe, in the long run, that you would be good for him, I would never consider remarriage.''

''I understand,'' she said softly. His son did not need her as she'd feared. Just the opposite, in fact. ''Thank goodness you can provide what he does need.''

''For that I am very thankful,'' he agreed, ''but many other parents cannot do the same for their children, so I've channeled millions into trying to change that and will continue to do so.''

She smiled. ''That's good.''

He shoved a hand through his hair and dropped it to his hip. ''I hadn't intended to raise this issue in quite this manner, you know, but I always meant to give you a clear understanding of the situation when the time was right. I see now that I left it too long, so I won't press you for a decision. You need time to assimilate all this.''

She'd assimilated enough to understand that Lucien needed her like he needed another hole in his head. She could do nothing but complicate his life! So why then did he want to marry her? The thought that he must really love her, love her in a way that she hadn't even considered possible before, nearly took her breath away. Some very big questions remained, however.

Could she cope with the difficulties that came with being a permanent part of Lucien Tyrone's life?

How naive she had been to think that this trip

wouldn't change her mind—or at least re-frame the problem.

He turned her toward the hallway, his arm resting lightly about her waist. "I suspect you could use a rest before lunch. Mother has no doubt put you in a separate room, and I won't interfere with that unless you want me to."

"Maybe it's best to just leave it as it is for now," she answered softly.

He nodded, not bothering to hide his disappointment but not making a big deal of it, either. After consulting a passing maid, he delivered her to her room. On the way they agreed that they didn't need to stay the night, so dinner would be eaten aboard the plane on the return trip. She managed to ignore the lavishness of her surroundings in order to rest and refresh herself, bathing and changing her clothes. She didn't even try to sleep.

Luncheon was a calm, pleasant affair on one of the many terraces, with Eugenia behaving as if nothing but pleasantries had passed between them to this point. Afterward, Avis spent the afternoon watching at a distance as Lucien interacted with his son, playing, laughing, coaxing, teaching, every action measured, every reaction countered with extreme purpose. The man had the patience of Job. He worked her into the situation with small waves and smiles and gentle, repeated instruction, but Nicholas refrained from all but the most cursory acknowledgment, and Avis realized that it could be that way for a very long time. She understood, too, that as Nico progressed, Lucien would need to spend more and more time with him.

He admitted over dinner that it was so. The unspoken implication was that, as his wife, she would be expected to interact more and more with the boy—and his grandmother—as well. It was definitely something to think about, and she couldn't deny a welling of the old fear at the thought. Unlike her situation with Kenneth, any commitment she made to Lucien Tyrone would naturally extend to the others in his life. She had been willing with Kenneth's family, but any involvement beyond the most cursory had been rebuffed. How perfectly ironic.

After dinner, Lucien suggested that she take the bed in the jet's rear compartment and get some rest. She saw the signs of fatigue in him, however, and insisted that he needed to lie down, too. "Just let me hold you," he said, "then I can rest."

She agreed, and a few minutes later closed her eyes to the deep, steady cadence of his breathing. They slept for the remainder of the trip. The limo delivered them to her door about a quarter of nine in the evening. Lucien had simply held her on the plane, but she knew that if she let him stay, they would end by making love. He knew it, too, and to her surprise, he backed away.

"I won't keep you. I've been putting off business elsewhere. This is a good time to take care of it."

She nodded, feeling at once grateful and oddly disappointed. Lucien was a man who fought for what he wanted. No one could doubt that. But had he battled to the end now before she could say that her own fight was won?

Sometimes it seemed that he could read her mind. He kissed her, then held her face in his hands, smiling down at her wistfully.

"You know," he said, "I haven't wanted to admit it even to myself, but it all comes down to just one thing—whether or not you really love me."

She opened her mouth. She did love him. She had no doubt of that now, if she ever had had, but could she love him as courageously, as fearlessly, as he demanded and deserved? She clamped her jaw on indecision. He laid his forehead against hers for a moment, then he turned and walked back to the limo. She had never felt more like crying in her life.

Chapter Fifteen

Avis looked at the colorful invitation affixed to her refrigerator door with a magnet shaped like a teacup. The tiny hand-painted piece of china reminded her of the cup of coffee Lucien had served her in the green room of the Tyrone mansion, and for a moment she was back there again, on the receiving end of his wry, encouraging smile. A vague sense of shame enveloped her. He had been willing to take on his mother and complicate the care of his son for love of her, but she had ignored him, inured herself against him. For fear. In the eight days that he had been gone, she had come to see what a timid, shallow creature she'd become, and she had waited anxiously for him to return and make his proposal.

But he hadn't come, and he hadn't called. Had he

given up on her? Or did he simply believe that she had given up on him?

She moved her attention from the magnet to the piece of paper beneath it. Sierra had obviously printed it on her home computer. A bright border of yellow and green baby rattles edged the pale blue paper, and large, dark-blue block letters announced a baby shower/barbecue on the following Saturday, beginning at five o'clock in the afternoon. The ''guys'' were urged to bring poker chips for a friendly tournament of cards, the winner of which would be awarded a prize. The ''gals'' were asked to bring a side dish or snack. She would go, of course, and take a big bowl of her favorite pasta salad, but the closer Saturday came, the more she did not want to go alone.

It was early on Wednesday morning. She had no idea where Lucien was, but she knew where she wanted him to be.

Her hand reached for the telephone mounted on the wall above the kitchen counter, but before she removed it from its cradle, she bowed her head. Hot tears filled her eyes, and an ache flowed through her chest, a longing which, once faced, burgeoned. Taking a deep breath, she raised her head, blinked and lifted the receiver to dial the number of his personal cell phone. She reached his message center, and this time she punched the button that would allow her to record.

''Lucien, please call me. I hoped I'd see you or at least hear from you by now. I–I want you to come home. I mean, to Texas. Please. I need you.''

She hung up and left the room, intending to get dressed for work. The phone rang before she reached the stairs. She whirled around, running back to the kitchen, illogically bypassing the phone in the living room.

"Hello," she gasped into the receiver that she plucked from the wall.

Lucien's voice spoke to her at once, sounding urgent. "What's wrong?"

She smiled, feeling foolish and happy at the same time. "Wrong?"

"You said you needed me."

Turning her back to the counter, she leaned against it. "I do. I need an escort for Saturday. For a baby shower."

"A *baby shower?*"

"Sure. You know, a party where you bring gifts to a couple expecting a baby."

Silence, then, "And who would this couple be?"

Was that hope she heard in his voice? She closed her eyes, remembering a time when she had desperately wanted children, believing that they would make her marriage worthwhile. She had never expected to revive that dream. Clearing her throat, she said, "My friends Val and Ian Keene. They're having a little boy, their first child, and we're giving them a shower."

"Ah. And you need an escort for this?"

"Well, it's an unusual baby shower, a couples kind of thing. The guys are going to grill something and play cards for prizes. Oh, you don't happen to have some poker chips lying around somewhere, do you?"

She heard the smile in his voice as he said, ''I think I can gather up a few.''

''Good. Then I'll see you, say between four and five Saturday afternoon?''

''I think I can manage that,'' he said softly.

She cradled the phone with both hands. ''I'm glad. I'm so glad.''

''It took you long enough,'' he said, but then he laughed.

''Yeah, it did,'' she admitted, laughing, too. ''Oh, I forgot to tell you, wear jeans.''

''Jeans again. All right. Whatever you want.''

She closed her eyes and thought, *I want you.* ''See you then,'' she said and hung up.

His hands were shaking. Beyond nervous this time, he could only hope that she was ready to yield, but he'd learned never to take anything for granted where Avis was concerned. He'd fought hard to give her the space she'd obviously needed in order to come to grips with their situation, and she had finally called— with the pretext of needing an escort to a baby shower, of all things, not that it mattered. She could've said that she needed a lightbulb changed and he'd have blazed a trail straight to her doorstep. He just hoped that this wasn't another of her attempts to hedge in and limit the relationship. One word that she'd said in her telephone message had encouraged him greatly. *Home.*

It was a word that he himself often used loosely, thoughtlessly, but he was very aware now that home was not a place for him. Home was people, Nico before this and now Avis.

The limo braked to a stop, and Lucien reached for the door handle. "Wait here, Jeff, until I know whether or not I'm going to need you again."

"Yes, sir."

Lucien got out of the car, carrying a bag containing a specially designed teddy bear garbed in fireman's gear and a matching suit of infant clothes, as well as a leather case containing personalized gambling chips. He walked toward her door. It opened just as he set foot on the bottom porch step, and he looked up into her beaming face. "You're here."

He smiled as he climbed the remaining two steps. "Yes."

She rocked up onto her tiptoes, eagerness muted by her natural reticence. Having none of that himself, he leaned forward and kissed her cheek. She lifted all the way up onto her toes and looped her arms around his neck.

"I've missed you."

He wrapped his arms around her, sorry that his hands were full but happy just to hold her again. "I've missed you, too."

She framed his face with her hands, leaned into him and kissed him on the mouth, bending one leg back at the knee. Then she literally bounced away and waved at Jeff, latching her other hand onto Lucien's. "Let's take my car."

"All right." Grinning, he signaled Jeff with a shooing motion and received a salute in reply. The limo was backing out of the drive as Avis pulled him into the house.

"Let me grab the gift and my purse. Oh, and there's a big bowl of pasta salad on the counter in the kitchen. Think you can manage that?"

"Sure." He watched her hurry into the living room, painfully aware that his hunger for her never seemed to abate. Any other time, he'd haul her up the stairs, baby shower be damned, but more was at stake here than a satisfying romp in her bed. Mentally sighing, he followed her through the house. She snatched up a large, elaborately wrapped box and her handbag on the way into the kitchen, while he followed, admiring the fit of her capri pants, which were simple khakis topped by a snug little T-shirt of deep green. She also wore tan, backless flats of canvas material, very casual yet somehow elegant. She could make a paper bag look elegant.

In the kitchen, she took his gift bag from him and held it in the same hand as her purse. "You didn't have to bring a present."

"But I wanted to," he said, placing the case containing the gambling chips atop the clear plastic lid on the big bowl of pasta salad. "Children deserve celebration. Besides, I want to make a good impression."

She rolled her eyes. "As if the Greek Tycoon could do anything else."

Grinning, he followed her through the utility room and out into the garage, carrying the bowl. She dropped down behind the steering wheel and shifted the gifts into the back, so he got into the passenger seat, holding the pasta salad and poker chips on his lap.

They headed west through town and out into the countryside. He was particularly interested in the out-lying area and observed the passing scenery with care, noting the rolling hills, flat fields and occasional outcroppings of rock punctuated by clumps of gnarly trees. They turned north for a bit and then pulled into the yard of an unusual compound consisting of a nice, new, fair-sized house built of stone and a number of odd outbuildings. Two proved to be elaborate green-houses, and two more, small barns, one of them quite distant. Beyond the buildings flowed regimented fields of flowers, but these were not the decorative, almost frivolous beds that his mother so loved. These looked much more like crops.

"Are they farming flowers here?" he asked with genuine surprise.

"They are, indeed," she told him with a smile. "Anything you want to know, just ask Sam. He tends to wax eloquent on the subject." Interesting.

She parked the car beside the house and bounced out, reaching into the back for the gifts. He got out on his side. "Let's walk around," she said over the top of the car. "The grill's on the back deck. Sam's very proud of his deck, by the way."

He followed her around the house, kicking up a fine, powdery dust along the way. A trio of children, all girls, burst out of a side door and ran laughing toward them. "Aunt Avis! Aunt Avis!"

He looked at her in surprise. "Your nieces?"

"Honorary," she managed before the girls

swamped her. Two of them, he noticed, were identical and younger than the third, who snatched the gifts from Avis's arms, saying she'd take them inside, while the others threw hugs at Avis.

"Everybody's in the back," the twins said in unison.

"That's where we're headed."

The twins peeled off and ran to deliver the news of their arrival, while the elder of the three disappeared into the house with the gifts. Avis linked her arm with Luc's and led him on. At the corner where the house met an enormous deck, they were met by a tall, slender woman with long, curly, red hair. She wore a sleeveless maternity top with cuffed shorts.

"You're early!" she exclaimed, coming down the steps to throw her arms around Avis. "And not alone." She drew back, one arm draped casually around Avis's neck, and blatantly took in Lucien. He inclined his head, smiling.

"This is Lucien Tyrone," Avis said, and the touch of pride in her voice widened his smile.

He shifted the bowl into the crook of one arm. "You must be Val."

The redhead rested her hand on her slightly protruding belly and laughed, shaking her head. "Wrong pregnant lady."

"This is our hostess Sierra Jayce," Avis said.

"Val is more pregnant than me—I mean, further along. Pregnant's pregnant, right?"

Lucien chuckled. "So it would seem. How do you do, Sierra Jayce. It's a pleasure to meet you."

"Ooh," Sierra commented, sliding a look at Avis, "Continental."

"Very," Avis said with a laugh.

Sierra waggled a brow suggestively, then bounded up the steps, saying, "Come and meet my husband. See if you can keep him from charring the steaks into charcoal briquets. He worries about bacteria."

"I'll do my best," Lucien promised, motioning for Avis to precede him up the short flight of stairs. As she did so, he yielded to temptation and patted her fanny. She shot him a look over her shoulder, laughed and hurried ahead. He was feeling very good.

Sam Jayce was younger than Lucien had expected but open and friendly, with a hearty handshake and enough politeness to temper his curiosity. As of yet, no steaks had been placed on the grill. In fact, he was just preparing to light the charcoal. "I thought about a gas grill," he said, "but it's just not the same, you know."

"Not at all," Lucien agreed. "Is that hickory wood you're adding?"

"Mesquite."

"Ah." Lucien sniffed a chunk of the wood. "I hope you're using a light marinade."

"Hmm," Sam said, rubbing his chin. "What would you suggest?"

Lucien shrugged and considered. "Beer?"

Sam grinned. "Wanna show me how it's done?"

"My pleasure."

They lit the charcoal, closed the lid and turned toward the house. The women were standing with their heads together, talking and watching. Avis smiled. He swept his fingers across her cheek as he passed her by.

The Jayces had a great kitchen, and Sam threw open the cabinets, laying it at Lucien's disposal as he talked about his family while Lucien began whipping up a beef marinade with spices pulled from the cabinet and a bottle of beer. Sam opened another for him to drink. He and Sierra were expecting their first child and were raising his twin sisters and Sierra's daughter from another marriage. Lucien felt comfortable enough with this man to ask, "How old are you?"

"Twenty-four."

"You're very mature."

Sam shrugged. "Life'll do that to you."

Luc nodded. "Yes, it will." He jerked a head toward the window over the sink. "Suppose you tell me about those flowers."

Sam was still telling him about those flowers when the guests of honor arrived, followed quickly by about a dozen other people, including a number of firefighters. Avis made a point of introducing him to a fit, ponytailed mother of two teenagers who treated him to a frank appraisal and finally announced, "Well, I knew he had to be something special."

"Thank you," he said, liking this blunt-spoken Gwyn immediately. In fact, he liked all of Avis's friends.

Sierra was warm and earthy, a little older than her obviously besotted husband. Sam stood up well next to Ian Keene, who was a big, commanding fellow, a man's man, so to speak, and a husband who couldn't seem to keep his eyes or his hands off his pert little wife. Something about Val made Lucien want to laugh. Maybe it was the quirky bleached hair or the body-hugging clothes that delineated every curve, including her bulging belly, with brash celebration. Or maybe it was the way she looked at her husband as if she could eat him.

The gathering was unlike any party he'd ever attended and yet, exactly the same. The attendees laughed and talked in constantly reconstituting groups, though the women generally fluttered around a cake and punch bowl while the men gravitated to a bag of potato chips and a cooler of beer. Cards broke out, and while the women opened and gushed over the gifts in the other room, Lucien amassed a huge pile of chips. None of the other men seemed to mind. It was all for fun, but when it came time for the steaks to go onto the grill and Sam asked for Luc's help with the cooking, the others sent him on his way with friendly cracks about how he must have amassed his fortune and how kind he was to leave the cheesy prizes for them.

"One must be mindful of one's duty to the cheesy," he quipped with a wink, and departed to hoots and laughter.

"Hey, you're all right," Sam announced as they walked away from the game table. He smacked Luc in the chest with the back of his hand as he spoke.

"Thanks," Luc replied dryly, and oddly enough it was one of the proudest moments of his very privileged and very experienced life.

Avis glanced at Lucien and Sam, standing side by side in front of an enormous grill, flipping steaks. Luc had donned one of Sam's white bib aprons, and the two appeared to be carrying on a laughing conversation. She shared a look with Sierra.

"Who'd have thought one of the richest men on earth would be so comfortable with my farmer husband and vice versa?"

Avis just smiled. Val, who had gone nuts over the fireman teddy bear and the tiny matching outfit, had her own comment. "Ian says he's a killer poker player and easily today's big winner, but that he's a good sport, too."

Avis was not surprised. In a very real sense, Lucien Tyrone played poker for a living. He gambled big on every enterprise and more often than not won big, big enough that the whole world knew how good he was at the game. The surprise was how well he seemed to fit in here. Oh, he was out of place to be sure, but he seemed content in that company and they in his. She felt gratified and not a little smug, to her own embarrassment.

When everyone else had been served their steaks, she accompanied Luc to the buffet spread out on a pair of rectangular picnic tables in the center of the huge deck. He clearly did not know what some of the dishes were, but he sampled a bit of everything and piled onto his plate whatever took his fancy, then they claimed one of the last chairs and briefly argued over who would sit in it. She finally plopped herself down on the deck, folded her legs, balanced her disposable plate on her knees and proceeded to eat. Luc took the chair with a sigh, and before she knew what was happening, he was back at the buffet refilling his plate.

He pronounced himself stuffed some time later and sprawled in the sloping Adirondack-style chair with his eyes closed. Avis leaned against his leg, listening to the ebb and flow of conversation around her until it was deemed time to cut the cake. She brought him a piece, and found him in conversation with Ian about the latter's duties as fire marshal. He smiled at her and patted the arm of his chair, so she perched herself there. He took a couple bites of the cake, then handed the plate back to her. She polished off the remainder while listening to Ian describe the heavy equipment owned and employed by his department. Luc seemed engrossed.

Gradually, the party began to break up in dribs and drabs, until only the guests of honor, their hosts, Luc, Avis and Gwyn remained, sitting beneath the stars with drinks in hand and full bellies. The girls had gone off to play under the watchful eyes of Gwyn's teenagers.

"I have some interesting news," Ian announced presently. "Heston Witt has resigned as mayor."

This was greeted by gasps. Lucien flicked a crumb of something off his jeaned thigh but said nothing.

Sierra and Sam leaned against the deck railing behind the chair that Ian had dragged over next to Luc's. Sierra lifted her head from Sam's shoulder. "Sweet heaven, you don't suppose we're actually shed of that vindictive worm, do you?"

"Could be," Gwyn said. "I heard he's sold the ranch."

"No kidding?" Sam exclaimed, his arms wrapped around Sierra's thickening waist. "I always figured he'd have to break it up in little pieces and sell it off over the years. Who would've bought the whole thing?''

Who indeed? Avis felt a jolt of certainty. She laid her hand on Lucien's shoulder. He covered it with his own but did not meet her gaze. Instead, he cleared his throat and addressed Sam's question. ''Someone willing to wager that a cheap parcel of land that size could be a good investment.''

It was all the confirmation she needed. Shocked, she asked, ''How cheap?''

He finally met her gaze. ''Cheap enough to be a bargain but still allow the mayor to retire to the Gulf coast in some comfort.''

''You bought it!'' Val exclaimed.

Lucien said nothing, just held Avis's gaze. His lack of denial was taken for confirmation.

''You interested in ranching?'' Ian asked.

''Not particularly,'' Lucien replied, ''but I am interested in making a home around here.''

Avis felt her chest tighten. Tears welled into her eyes. Was there no end to what this man would do for her? She had never even imagined this kind of love, his kind of love, but now she was through with doubts and foolish fears. She was ready to grab happiness with both hands.

''Luc and I are getting married,'' she announced, looking into his dark eyes.

All the air rushed out of his lungs in a great *whoosh,* and he hauled her off the arm of his chair and onto his lap, kissing her face, burying his in the curve of her neck.

"I love you," he whispered.

"I know."

He lifted his head. "I'll never cage you, I swear. You'll make your own decisions, have your own life, whatever you need."

She covered his mouth with her fingertips. "I know."

"I'll build you a big house right in the middle of all that land."

"And put a fence around it," she added.

"*And* keep you chained to the bed until you give me babies," he warned with a broad grin.

She cast a sly, pleased look around. "Rubbed off on you, have they?"

He shook his head. "No, that was you, but they certainly make an excellent argument for wedded bliss and parenthood, don't they?"

"They certainly do." She glanced at Sierra and added, "Sometimes too good." She looped her arms around his neck then and promised, "I'll be a good mother, whatever that takes. Oh, and I'll also put up with yours."

He reared his head back and laughed in great, ringing shouts. "Now that's true love!"

"It certainly is," she agreed wryly.

Grinning so broadly that it must have hurt, he stood with her in his arms, and was instantly mobbed by the three other women present. They hugged and laughed and gushed delight over the engagement. It was Gwyn, though, whose tears most moved Avis. She wrapped one arm around her friend's neck and held on tight. When she finally pulled back, a silent message passed between them. Of the four friends who had struggled so to make their livings in that decrepit little strip mall on the edge of Puma Springs, only Gwyn had not inherited, and only Gwyn remained alone. It felt terribly unfair to Avis, but Gwyn was strong, and her delight for Avis shone in her eyes.

Luc took that opportunity to say to the group at large, "Good evening, friends. It's been great, but we're going home now."

Avis shocked herself by waggling an eyebrow suggestively at her friends, and knowing laughter erupted. As Luc carried her across the deck, Sam called out teasingly, "Hey, you forgot your poker chips."

"Keep them, with my compliments."

"You forgot your prize, too," Sierra said.

"No, I didn't," Luc said, looking down at Avis.

She curled her arms around his neck and said, "I do love you."

"I cannot doubt it," he replied, quickly taking the steps down to the ground, "but I'll let you prove it to me just the same."

Laughing happily, she felt light as air, no longer encumbered by regret or uncertainty. An image flashed before her mind's eye: Edwin Searle, gnarled and bent, a cowboy hat clasped in one hand, the other clasping that of his beloved wife. They looked at one another, and then they looked down, and Edwin nodded with satisfaction. Avis imagined that they were looking down from the clouds on her and Luc, and her heart swelled with gratitude and joy. Sure and brave, she let herself be carried into the future on a wave of pure love.

*   *   *   *   *

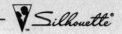

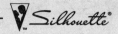

SPECIAL EDITION™

Susan Mallery

presents the continuation
of the bestselling series

DESERT ROGUES

Watch how passion flares under the hot desert sun for these rogue sheiks!

THE SHEIK & THE PRINCESS IN WAITING
(Silhouette Special Edition #1606)

Prince Reyhan had been commanded by his father,
the king of Bahania, to marry as befit his position.
There was just one tiny matter in the way:
divorcing his estranged wife Emma Kennedy.
Seeing the lovely Emma again brought back
a powerful attraction...and a love long buried.
Could Reyhan choose duty over his heart's desire?

Available April 2004 at your favorite retail outlet.

If you enjoyed what you just read,
then we've got an offer you can't resist!

Take 2 bestselling
love stories FREE!
Plus get a FREE surprise gift!

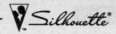

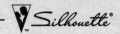

SPECIAL EDITION™

MILLION DOLLAR DESTINIES

Three brothers discover
all the riches money can't buy.

**A delightful new series
from *USA TODAY* bestselling author**

SHERRYL WOODS

ISN'T IT RICH?
(Silhouette Special Edition #1597, on sale March 2004)

PRICELESS
(Silhouette Special Edition #1603, on sale April 2004)

TREASURED
(Silhouette Special Edition #1609, on sale May 2004)

And don't miss...

DESTINY UNLEASHED
a *Million Dollar Destinies* story
on sale June 2004 from MIRA Books.

Available at your favorite retail outlet.

COMING NEXT MONTH

SPECIAL EDITION